Ernest Axon

**Family of Bayley of Manchester and Hope**

Ernest Axon

**Family of Bayley of Manchester and Hope**

ISBN/EAN: 9783337092108

Printed in Europe, USA, Canada, Australia, Japan

Cover: Foto ©Andreas Hilbeck / pixelio.de

More available books at **www.hansebooks.com**

THE

# FAMILY OF BAYLEY

## OF MANCHESTER AND HOPE.

BY

### ERNEST AXON.

MANCHESTER: PRINTED FOR THE AUTHOR.
1894.

# PREFACE.

THE following account of the family of Bayley of Manchester and Hope was originally reprinted from the *Transactions of the Antiquarian Society of Lancashire and Cheshire* for 1889, and is now re-issued at the request of several members of the family. It has been rearranged and is so much enlarged that it is practically a new work. The author has to express his thanks to the members of the family who have kindly assisted him, and especially to Lady BAYLEY, the widow of Sir EDWARD CLIVE BAYLEY, K.C.S.I., Mrs. EDWARD BAYLEY, Mrs. MACNAMARA, Mrs. JOHN ARTHUR FOWLER, Mrs. J. A. HARRIS, Sir STEUART COLVIN BAYLEY, K.C.I.E., Mr. THOMAS BAYLEY POTTER, M.P., the late Dr. W. C. HENRY, F.R.S., and Mr. FRANCIS S. BAYLEY. Mr. W. A. SHAW, M.A., Mr. T. CANN HUGHES, M.A., and Mr. JOHN OWEN have also rendered assistance. To Sir STEUART BAYLEY the author is also indebted for the opportunity of reproducing, as a frontispiece, the view of Hope Hall as it existed in the time of Thomas Butterworth Bayley.

23, SHAW ROAD,
HEATON MOOR,
Stockport.

BAYLEY ARMS.

ARMS: Argent, on a fesse between three martlets gules
as many plates.

CREST: A griffin sejant ermine, winged and armed or.

MOTTO: "Deus pro nobis quis contra nos."

# THE FAMILY OF BAYLEY, 1894.

## CORRECTION.

page vii.   For  "MOTTO: 'Deus pro nobis quis contra nos.'"
Read "MOTTO: 'Quicquid agas, age pro viribus.'"

# CONTENTS.

HOPE HALL IN THE TIME OF T. B. BAYLEY, ESQ.  *Frontispiece.*

PREFACE - - - - - - - v

BAYLEY ARMS - - - - - - vii

CONTENTS - - - - - - - viii

PEDIGREE A.—BAYLEY FAMILY, ELDEST LINE - 1

PEDIGREE B.—W. B. BAYLEY AND HIS DESCENDANTS - 32

PEDIGREE C.—BAYLEY OF WITHINGTON - - 38

PEDIGREE D.—BAYLEY OF BOOTH HALL - - 42

PEDIGREE E.—JAMES BAYLEY, OF MANCHESTER, AND HIS
                    DESCENDANTS - - - 46

BIBLIOGRAPHICAL APPENDIX - - - - 51

NOTES - - - - - - - 56
            (1) AUTHORITIES.
            (2) ORIGIN OF THE FAMILY.

INDEX - - - - - - - 57

# The Bayley Family.

## A.—BAYLEY OF MANCHESTER AND HOPE.

### I.

THOMAS BAYLEY, of Deansgate, Manchester, silk weaver.[1] From 1647 to 1679 he acted frequently as an office holder under the Court Leet, as officer for mastiff dogs and for forestallers and regrators of the market, as market looker for white meat, as mise gatherer, and in various other capacities. In 1651 and several later years he was one of the jury.[2] In 1661 he took the oath of allegiance, and in 1668 was assessed at 1s. 4d. for his house in Deansgate. He was buried at the Collegiate Church, 28th August, 1688. His administration bond, preserved at Chester, is printed below:—

> Bond by which Ann Bayley of Manchester, co. Lanc. widow, and George Warburton of Manchester aforesaid, are bound to the Bishop of Chester, in £80. Dated 25th August 1693
>
> The condition is that the above bounden Ann Bayley, administratrix of all the goods, &c. of her late husband Thomas Bayley of Manchester, aforesaid, silk weaver, deceased, do make or cause to be made and exhibited

---

[1] "Silk weaver" was the seventeenth century equivalent of "silk manufacturer."

[2] Earwaker's *Court Leet Records*, iv., v., vi.

B

a true Inventory of all the goods, &c of the said deceased,
at or before the 10th Dec. next ensuing

    Sealed and delivered

    in the presence of,

        Ric: Wroe        Ann Bayley

        Sam^ll Wrightson    her A B mark

                      George Warburton

Inventory taken 22 Aug^st 1693 by Joseph Bradshaw
and Thomas Anderson.

    Household goods &c, In the House, Buttery,
Parlour, Chamber, Backside.   Total 13^li. 4^s 11^d

Exhibited 25 Aug^st 1693

Thomas Bayley married at the Collegiate Church,
26th August, 1641,[1] Ann Churton, probably one of the
family of Chorlton, by whom he had seven children, all
of whom were baptized at the Collegiate Church:—

1. ANNE, bap. 17th July, 1642; bur. at Collegiate Church,
15th August, 1649.

2. ALICE, bap. 8th September, 1644; married at Collegiate
Church, 8th September, 1664, to Theophilus Astle.

3. TIMOTHY, bap. 28th December, 1645; bur. 19th January,
1646-7.

4. THOMAS, bap. 6th June, 1647.

5. SARAH, bap. March, 1649-50; bur. 24th March, 1649-50.

6. DANIEL, of whom presently.

7. MARY, bap. 13th April, 1659; bur. 28th August, 1660.


## II.

DANIEL BAYLEY, of Manchester, silk weaver.  Baptized
at the Collegiate Church, 26th October, 1651.  In 1679,
1683, and 1684, he was appointed respectively an inmates

---

[1] All baptisms, marriages, and burials at the Collegiate Church are
from Mr. Owen's transcripts, unless otherwise stated.

officer for Markett Street Lane, bylaw man for Deansgate, and market looker for weights and measures. In 1684 he was fined for not keeping in repair the street before his house.[1] He died before his father, his death being referred to by the Rev. Henry Newcome,[2] under date 23rd February, 1684-5: "Dan Bayley died this morning." He was buried at the Collegiate Church on the following day. Administration to his estate was granted 14th March, 1684-5, to "Sara Baley widow, relict of the deceased."

Daniel Bayley was married by licence, dated 25 Car. II. and filed at Chester,[3] to Sarah, daughter of the Rev. James Bradshaw, of Darcy Lever. She was baptized at Wigan, 15th September, 1650.[4] After the death of her husband she appears to have continued his business. She is mentioned in the Court Leet Records in 1686 and 1687, and on 22nd May, 1690, was assessed at o. 1. o. for the poll tax.[5] She was buried in the Collegiate Church, 30th July, 1695, and her will, dated 26th April, 1695, was proved at Chester on 14th August following.

The children of Daniel and Sarah Bayley were:—

1. JAMES, of whom presently.

2. ELIZABETH, bap. 17th February, 1675-6, at Collegiate Church.

3. ANNE, bap. 21st November, 1678, at Collegiate Church.

4. SARAH, bap. 21st April, 1681, at Collegiate Church.

5. ALICE, bap. 10th April, 1684; bur. 7th May, 1696;[6] both at the Collegiate Church.[7]

---

[1] *Court Leet Records*, vi.
[2] *Autobiography*, ii. 306.
[3] *Local Gleanings.*
[4] Bridgeman's *Church of Wigan*, iii. 470.
[5] *Pole Booke for Manchester* (Chet. Soc., lvii.).
[6] Bailey's pedigree says 1695.
[7] One of the daughters married a Mr. Stott, of Manchester.

## III.

JAMES BAYLEY, of Manchester, merchant.  He was
baptized at the Collegiate Church, 4th February, 1673-4.
In 1703 he was churchwarden.[1]  In 1721 he was one of
the undertakers for making the Mersey and Irwell navigable.[2]  At the time of the rebellion, in 1745, he was the
oldest and one of the most prosperous of the Manchester
merchants, and, as he was also a Whig, he was amongst
those to whom, on 9th December, 1745, the young Pretender, then on his retreat from Derby, addressed a
warrant "to raise from the town £5,000 against the next
day by four o'clock on pain of military execution."  It
was thought impossible to do this considering the sums,
amounting to nearly £3,000, that had been extorted from
the town before.  Next morning, 10th December, 1745, a
number of the inhabitants "waited on the Pretender to
acquaint him with the impossibility of raising the money,
and to endeavour to have the payment excused.  Upon
this he mitigated it to £2,500, and sent a warrant for that
sum to be levied upon Manchester and Salford by one
o'clock; and while methods were being contrived how to
procure it, three or four of the rebels seized Mr. James
Bailey, senior, took him to Secretary Murray at the
Pretender's lodgings, and told him he must be prisoner
till it was paid; and if it was not paid he must go with
them.  Mr. Bailey excused himself by saying he was
betwixt seventy and eighty years old, and, to his remem-
brance, had not lain a night out of his own bed for two

---

[1] Harland's *Court Leet Records*, i. 196.
[2] Baines's *Liverpool*, p. 402.

years, nor could bear travel. He was told, if he could not ride, they would endeavour to get him a wheel carriage. Mr. Bailey said his confinement was an obstruction to the raising of the money, and that if he was at liberty he might borrow some. The Secretary brought an answer, that the Prince, in consideration of his age, if he would give him his word and honour to fetch him £2,500 in two hours or surrender himself a prisoner, consented he should have his liberty so long. This Mr. Bailey agreed to, and went to the coffee-house where a great number of the inhabitants were; and it being proposed that Mr. Bailey and Mr. Dickinson should give promissary notes, payable in three months, to such as would lend any money; it was agreed to, and the money being thereby procured was paid about two o'clock."[1]

Dr. Byrom's journals give a similiar account of the matter, though it has been said by some writers that Mr. Bayley was seized by the rebels when on their way to Derby, and that he was not released until their retreat. Mr. Bayley is sometimes described as of Hope Hall, but it is doubtful if he ever resided there. As late as 1744 Mr. Thomas Bradshaw is given in a list of ley payers as the occupant of Hope.[2] There is no doubt that for the greater part of his life he resided in Bayley's Court, Market Place. His house there is no longer standing, but Mr. John Owen saw it in 1864, and has kindly given me this description: "At the bottom of this Court is a tolerably large house of brick, three stories in height,

---

[1] Ray's *History of the Rebellion*, pp. 101-102.
[2] Harland's *Parish Church of Eccles*, p. 55.

exclusive of the cellar, the stories being divided by a couple
of plain stone string-courses.  The front has five windows
to each story, except the lower one, which has the door-
way in the centre under a round arch; the windows have
flat arches of brick, and appear to be twice as long as
broad.   In some of them are the original framework,
having a central mullion or stanchion with a transom in
the upper part.   The eaves project considerably, supported by brackets, and immediately underneath is a
border of ornamental plaisterwork.   The base of the
building, to a height of about three feet, is of stone and
weathered.   On the leaden spout which is against the face
of the building is the following inscription, I$^B$S 1707,
the initials of James and Sarah Bayley.   The entrance
leads to a square oak staircase, and the internal walls
are of timber and plaister."   James Bayley died on the
6th April, 1753, and was buried in the north aisle of the
chancel of the Collegiate Church.

James Bayley married on 3rd January, 1698, Sarah,
daughter of Samuel Kirkes, of Chester.   Mrs. Bayley
was buried 8th January, 1719-20, at the Collegiate
Church.

The children of James and Sarah Bayley were:—

1. DANIEL, of whom presently.

2. SAMUEL, bap. 16th December, 1701; bur. at Collegiate
Church, 4th January, 1701-2.

3. JAMES, of whom below (Pedigree C).

4. JOHN, bap. 23rd February, 1707-8; bur. 1st July, 1709.

5. SARAH, born 12th May, bap. 22nd May, 1710; married
4th March, 1734, at the Collegiate Church, to John Touchet,
of Manchester, merchant, and one of the trustees of Cross
Street Chapel.   From this marriage descended, amongst

others, Hannah Touchet, wife of Archdeacon Bayley,
William Harrison Ainsworth, the novelist, J. Bower
Harrison, M.D., the Rev. John Harrison, Ph.D., the late
Mrs. ffarington, of Worden, and Mrs. Nicholas J. Ridley.

6. MARY, bur. 29th March, 1713.

7. SAMUEL, of whom presently (Pedigree D).

8. BENJAMIN, bur. 28th September, 1722.

## IV.

DANIEL BAYLEY, of Hope Hall, eldest son of James
and Sarah Bayley, was born 13th October, 1699. He
seems to have been at an early age associated with his
father in business, and in 1721 was one of the undertakers for making the rivers Mersey and Irwell navigable.
It is probable that he retired while still a young man.
In 1732, when he was described as "gentleman," he was
appointed a trustee of Cross Street Chapel, where he was
a regular attendant, and remained in the trust until his
death. In June, 1749, Daniel Bayley went to reside at
Hope Hall, in the parish of Eccles, a property which had
belonged to his distant kinsfolk the Bradshaws, and a
few years later rebuilt it on the old foundations. He is
said to have been a deputy-lieutenant for the county,[1]
and he served occasionally as a grand juryman at the
Lancaster assizes. He took an interest in science, and
under his auspices and on his estate Samuel Smethurst
and Peter Clare observed in 1761 the transit of Venus.
Eight years later the hall was again placed at their
disposal for a similar purpose by Daniel Bayley's son.
Daniel Bayley was an energetic Dissenter; his name

---

[1] Baker's *Memorials of a Dissenting Chapel*, p. 79.

appears first of those appended to the circular calling the
first general meeting for the foundation of the Warrington Academy, and he gave £100 to be held on the same
trusts as the £500 which had been given by his wife's
grandmother, Ann Butterworth, for binding apprentice
the children of poor Protestant Dissenting ministers and
decayed tradesmen.    He died 14th May, 1764, and is
said to have been buried in a vault he had made in Hart's
Hill Meadow, behind Hope Hall, and to have been subsequently interred in the family vault in Eccles Church.
In opposition to this it is stated by Sir Thomas Baker[1]
that he was buried in Cross Street Chapel, where "the
words on the stone are not 'In memory of,' &c., but
'Here lie the remains of,' &c."

Daniel Bayley was twice married.  His first wife,
whom he married in 1717,[2] was Elizabeth, daughter and
coheiress of Nathaniel Gaskell, of Manchester.    Mrs.
Bayley's two sisters married respectively Hugh, eleventh
Lord Sempill, and Richard Clive, M.P., of Styche.  Mrs.
Clive's son, Robert, afterwards the celebrated Lord Clive,
lived for several years with Mr. and Mrs. Daniel Bayley,
at Manchester, and was trained and educated by Mr.
Bayley as though he had been his own son.  At the end
of 1728 the little fellow, then only two years old, had a
dangerous attack of fever, on which occasion Mr. Bayley
wrote to Styche: "Thank God, I do now inform you
that Bob continues better, and is in a very likely way to
recover.  We hope that the crisis of the fever was on

---

[1] *Memorials of a Dissenting Chapel*, p. 79.
[2] *Northowram Registers*, p. 212.

Saturday last, about noon, it having abated ever since.
His exceeding patience is also exchanged for as eminent
a degree of crossness, which we take as a good omen of
his mending. I am writing this close to his bedside, and
he is crying with the greatest impatience for me to be on
the bed with him; nor will he be quiet one moment, with
all the fine words I can give him, which now makes me
conclude abruptly." Young Clive had a relapse, but by
January he was well again, and "with some reluctance
suffered his Aunt Bay to go to Chapel." The chapel here
mentioned is the Presbyterian, now Unitarian, Chapel in
Cross Street, Manchester, at which the Bayley family
were at that time regular attendants, and of which
Nathaniel Gaskell, Clive's grandfather, was one of the
founders, and is named first in the earliest trust deed. In
1732 Mr. Bayley wrote: "I hope I have made a little
further conquest over Bob, and that he regards me in
some degree as well as his Aunt Bay. He has just had a
new suit of clothes, and promises by his reformation to
deserve them. I am satisfied that his fighting (to which
he is out of measure addicted) gives his temper a fierce-
ness and imperiousness, and he flies out upon trifling
occasion; for this reason I do what I can to suppress the
hero, that I may help forward the valuable qualities of
meekness, benevolence, and patience. I assure you, sir,
it is a matter of concern to us, as it is of importance to
himself, that he may be a good and virtuous man, to
which no care of ours shall be wanting." Plassy showed
that the worthy uncle was unable to "suppress the hero"
in his young charge. Long afterwards, when Clive was
far away in India, his thoughts would turn back to his

C

pleasant Lancashire home, to the unpretending chapel
frequented by his Presbyterian relatives, to his juvenile
encounters and battles, and to all the other circumstances
that made him sigh for what, in one of his letters, he calls
"dear, delightful Manchester." In another letter he
says, "If I could be so far blest as to revisit again my
own country, but more especially Manchester, the centre
of all my wishes, and all that I could hope for or desire
would be presented before me in one view." Mr. Bayley
lived long enough to see Clive the most famous man of
his age. Mrs. Bayley died 26th February, 1734-5, in her
thirty-fifth year, and on the 12th April following her only
child, Elizabeth, died, aged two. Mother and child were
buried in the Collegiate Church, Manchester.

Mr. Daniel Bayley's second wife was Anne, daughter
and coheiress (with her sisters, Lady Hoghton and Mrs.
Joddrell, afterwards the Hon. Mrs. George Sempill) of
Thomas Butterworth, of Manchester, gentleman, by his
wife, Frances, daughter of Sir Robert Dukinfield, baronet.
Mr. Butterworth's father, Thomas Butterworth, was a
leading Manchester merchant, and had married Ann
Crowther, a niece of Sir Edward Mosley, of Hulme,
knight, and a cousin of Sir Robert Booth, lord chief justice of the common pleas in Ireland. Mrs. Bayley was
born 25th March, 1713, and was married 24th June,
1736. At her marriage she had not been dealt with
by father so generously as her sister Lady Hoghton,
who had a marriage portion of £8,000, but her father,
who died in 1745, by his will dated 25th December,
1744, made further provision for her, as is shown by
the following abstracts: "To his daughter Anne wife of

Mr Daniel Bayley, he had already given £3800 and
he now further bequeaths for life  All those two messuages or dwelling houses with the appurtenances situate
and being near the Cross in Manchester aforesaid in the
several occupations of John Berry & John Bracegirdle
or their respective Undertenants  Also all those two
Messuages or dwelling Houses with the app$^s$ situate
& being in a certain street called the Smithy Door in
Manchester aforesaid in the several occupations of
Richard Jackson and Magdalene Whitworth widow or
their respective Undertenants  And also all my Messuages
Farmes and Tenements lying and being in Chadderton
in the said County of Lancaster with the Lands &
Hereditaments thereunto respectively belonging or there-
with respectively occupied & enjoyed  And also that
Yearly Rent or sum of Two Pounds issuing or payable
out of a Messuage & Lands near Coleshau in Chadderton aforesaid  And also all those two other Messuages
or dwelling Houses with the Gardens Stables and
Appurtenances thereunto belonging or therewith respectively occupied & enjoyed at or near a place called
Tinker Lane within Oldham in the said County of
Lancaster now in the occupation of Samuel Taylor and
John Lees or their respective undertenants," with re-
mainder to Thomas Butterworth Bayley, the second son,
and heirs (the first son being provided for).  "Also I
give & bequeath all those my Messuages and Lands
situate in or near a certain Street called Deansgate in
Manchester aforesaid & also my Messuage & Lands in
Newton in the Parish of Manchester aforesaid (which
Messuage & Lands I hold by three several Leases for

years from the Warden & Fellows of the Collegiate Church of Manch[r] aforesaid) unto my said daughter Anne for life—and to any child she may limit"—her Ex[rs] &c.

"Also I give unto my said dāur Anne £80 due to me upon Mortgage from Jacob Taylor of Chadderton aforesaid." Residue amongst 3 Daughters equally.

"Executors my beloved son in law Daniel Bayley, my beloved brother in law Robert Dukinfield Esq[r] & my beloved friend & neighbour John Smith merchant. Signed in presence of Sam[l] Bayley Robert Hibbert jun[r] Judith Clough."[1]

Mrs. Bayley survived her husband thirty years. In her later years she lived in a house at the corner of St. Ann's Square (on the site now occupied by Heywood's Bank), which had been her father's. Her stately manners made such an impression on the youthful mind of Samuel Hibbert Ware, the antiquary, whose father lived opposite to Mrs. Bayley, that in after years whenever he met any severe-looking old lady he would style her "Madam Bayley."[2] She died at St. Ann's Square, 3rd March, 1795, aged eighty-two, and was buried at Cross Street. Daniel and Anne (Butterworth) Bayley had issue:—

1. James, born 5th April, 1737; died 3rd July, 1746, aged ten; bur. at Cross Street.

2. Frances, born 15th April, 1738; died 3rd May, 1742, aged five; bur. at Cross Street.

---

[1] From the transcript formerly in the possession of my friend the late John Eglington Bailey, F.S.A.

[2] *Life of S. Hibbert Ware.*

3. SARAH, born 19th April, 1741; died 16th November, 1743, aged three; bur. at Cross Street.

4. THOMAS BUTTERWORTH, of whom presently.

5. SUSANNAH, born 2nd April, 1746; died 28th December, 1755, aged eight; bur. at Cross Street.

6. DANIEL BENJAMIN, born 26th March, 1753; died 5th December, 1755, aged two; bur. at Cross Street.

## V.

THOMAS BUTTERWORTH BAYLEY, the only survivor of the children of Daniel Bayley, was born at Manchester, 20th June, 1744, and was educated at Edinburgh University. Shortly after succeeding his father, he was sworn a justice of the peace for the county of Lancaster, and he threw himself into his magisterial work with great energy. At the early age of twenty-four he was appointed high sheriff, and for a number of years he acted as chairman of quarter sessions, and as receiver of duchy rents. He was elected F.R.S., 18th February, 1773. In 1774 he offered himself as a candidate for the borough of Liverpool, but did not go to the poll.[1]

Of course so prominent a magistrate could not escape the Rev. Thomas Seddon when he was looking round for victims to impale in the *Characteristic Strictures*. Consequently he appears in that interesting work, published in 1779, as follows :—

> "Thomas B. B—ley, Esq., Hope.
> The figure of Hope.

"Among the various attempts of this artist we have not seen one tolerable performance. Had he modestly

---

[1] *Liverpool Weekly Magazine*, October 6th, 1774, p. 24.

confined himself to single figures he might probably have
been more successful; to represent numbers is infinitely
superior to his powers. We cannot, however, give him
much credit for this figure; the attitude is too presump-
tive for Hope and the cable too slender for the weight of
the anchor."

And in a foot note Seddon says: "His ambition has
led him to offer himself a candidate for several boroughs
in the county, but these and many other examples of
Quixotism, with a variety of curious anecdotes, will be
particularly described in the history of his life, which is
speedily to be published." Seddon refers to him again
in ironical terms in the dedication of a sermon printed in
1780; but what was the nature of the quarrel between
the clergyman and magistrate I have not been able
to ascertain.[1]    Bayley took part in all the patriotic

---

[1] It is interesting to compare the three following dedications to
Butterworth Bayley:—

"To Thomas Butterworth Bayley, Esq.; High-Sheriff of the County
Palatine of Lancaster, the following Essay is with the highest Respect,
for his Distinguished Abilities, and the sincerest Esteem, for his Amiable
Character, inscribed by his affectionate, and most obedient Servant

"THOMAS PERCIVAL."

(Percival's *Experiments and Observations on Water*, 1769.)

"To Thomas Butterworth Bayley, Esq., of Hope,
        "Fellow of the Royal Society.

"Sir,—It gives me the highest Satisfaction and Pleasure, that you have
condescended to receive this my first Essay under your Protection. And
all who are honoured with your Friendship, and are acquainted with your
superior knowledge in polite and useful Learning, in which you have
justly included the Science of Numbers, will be sensible of my Happiness
in being thus permitted to address you.

"Were my Abilities, Sir, equal to my Wishes, I could with Pleasure
dilate on those excellent Qualifications, adorned with the utmost Good-
nature and Humanity, which have rendered your Character so conspicuous. But, as I well know I should fail in the attempt, the only Use
I can make of this opportunity, is, to testify my Regard to so generous a

efforts in the neighbourhood, and no scheme for the amelioration of the condition of the people was carried out without his assistance. In 1782 he was lieutenant-colonel of the Manchester Military Association. In 1797 he took an active part in raising the Manchester and Salford Volunteers, subscribing twenty guineas towards

---

Patron, by publicly acknowledging the many Favours which I, however undeserving, have received at your Hands, and which I shall always remember with the sincerest gratitude.—I am, Sir, your most obliged and obedient Servant, "HENRY CLARKE."
(Dr. Henry Clarke's *Rationale of Circulating Numbers*, 1777.)

"To Thomas Butterworth Bayley, Esq.

"To introduce a publication of a political nature to the world, under the protection of a Great Man, is to ensure it a general reading by the Publick.—I therefore humbly dedicate the following Declamation to my most worthy Friend, Mr. Bayley,—trusting on his neighbourly affection to support me against the malignity of partial Commentators, or the attacks of dissatisfied Fanatics; and I am the more inclined to confide in this expectation, from the many observations made upon his publick, as well as private Conduct, both which declare his sincere attachment to the King and dutiful attention to the privileges of the Crown.

"As a Magistrate,—his Worship is so strenuous a defender of the Laws, that even those which are generally esteemed lenient,—when dealt out with his spirited exertion,—have in their consequences,—by moderate Men,—unwittingly been called severe.

"As a private Gentleman, he is so indefatigable to rectify every Grievance, that even the shadow of complaint cannot escape him, for with becoming activity he investigates the cupboard of every cottager in his neighbourhood,—with a manifest intention to suppress Luxury in its infancy, knowing by Family experience, that Æs in presenti perfectum format, and how difficult it is to soar above the loathsome Habitation of a Cellar,—without Temperance and Industry.

"From the above considerations I am persuaded, Mr. Bayley will not be displeased with this, tho' hasty attempt to vindicate the rights of Majesty, and to give evidence against the Stratagems of Treason, especially as it will discover to him a wish,—to follow his own laudable example of extracting another Name from deep obscurity.

"I am with much Gratitude, for the unmerited favours Mr. Bayley has so repeatedly conferred upon me, his most oblig'd and very humble Servant,

"Acres Barn, near Manchester, } "THOMAS SEDDON.
February 15th, 1780." }
(Seddon's *Sermon at Hardwick*, 1780.)

the initial expenses,[1] and becoming colonel of the regiment on its embodiment. The work in which he took the greatest interest, however, was the improvement of prisons. An earnest disciple of John Howard, he became convinced of the necessity for a prison on the modern plan to replace the old House of Correction, which was then in a disgraceful condition. With characteristic energy he overcame all opposition to his project; a site was selected, and in 1787 Mr. Bayley laid the first stone of the New Bayley Prison.[2] In 1790 the place was finished, but when, as chairman of quarter sessions, Mr. Bayley charged the grand jury, he had to speak of the death of Howard only a few weeks before the completion of one of the earliest of the prisons constructed in entire accordance with his views. The name of the prison has excited some discussion; the question in dispute is whether it is called the New Bailey after the Old Bailey in London, or whether it owed its name as well as existence to Mr. Butterworth Bayley. That during Mr. Bayley's lifetime the name was usually spelled as he spelled his name there can be no doubt, but it is equally certain that the next chairman of quarter sessions, who did not share Mr. Bayley's political views, was disinclined to allow the honour of the name to his Whig predecessor, and always insisted that the gaol was named after the prison in London and not after Mr. Bayley.[3]

In 1794, the grand jury, of which Mr. Bayley was foreman, requested the high sheriff to make efforts for

---

[1] *Manchester Mercury*, 7th March, 1797.
[2] Baines's *Lancashire*, edited by Croston, ii. 140.
[3] *Gentleman's Magazine*, 1819, vol. ii., 224, 386.

the amelioration of the condition of the debtors in Lancaster Gaol.[1] In 1796 Mr. Bayley was elected president of the newly-formed Manchester Board of Health.[2] Working on the lines of a plan drawn up at his request by Dr. John Ferriar, the board established the House of Recovery, an institution now amalgamated with the Royal Infirmary. Mr. Bayley was one of the first vice-presidents of the Literary and Philosophical Society,[3] and was the first promoter of the Manchester Humane Society in 1791; and when, in 1787, a society was formed in Manchester for the purpose of effecting the abolition of the slave trade, he and his mother were amongst the subscribers, and Mr. Bayley was elected a member of the first committee of the society.[4] It is worth mentioning that so early as 1788 Mr. Bayley advocated the substitution of paid constables for the then universal honorary constables.[5]

Mr. Bayley's leisure was devoted to agriculture, and it is to him that we owe the elms at Hope Hall. He was one of the founders of the Manchester Agricultural Society, and was awarded, by that society, several premiums; and he was an honorary member of the Board of Agriculture in London. Thomas B. Bayley was the author of several pamphlets, principally on agricultural topics, a list of which will be found in the appendix. Mr. Bayley's religious beliefs were broad. He was from 1778 to 1802 a

---

[1] *Preston Guardian Local Sketches*, 23rd May, 1883.
[2] *Proceedings of the Board of Health in Manchester.*
[3] Smith's *Centenary of Science.*
[4] *Manchester Mercury*, 15th January, 1798.
[5] *Manchester Mercury*, 7th October, 1788.

trustee of Cross Street Chapel,[1] and he was also a vice-president of the Warrington Academy.[2] It is related that on the occasion of the presentation of colours to the regiment, of which Mr. Bayley was colonel, there was a religious service at St. Ann's. It happened to be St. Matthew's Day, when the Athanasian Creed is appointed to be read in churches. Mr. Hall, in deference to the Presbyterian colonel, omitted this portion of the service, an action which lost Mr. Hall the chaplaincy of the Collegiate Church, which became vacant about that time.[3] He was an original seatholder and trustee of St. John's, Deansgate, the first incumbent of which was an earnest Swedenborgian.[4] Mr. Bayley was also an attendant at Eccles Church. Charles Hulbert, in his *Memoirs of an Eventful Life*, says: "I remember with reverence that worthy magistrate, chairman of the Salford quarter sessions, Thomas Butterworth Bayley, Esq. The first sermon for a Sunday school that I ever heard was at Eccles Church, when the justice bare-headed took his place at the church door with his box in his hand, repeatedly soliciting the congregation as it passed him, 'To remember the poor,' 'Do remember the poor.'"

Thomas Butterworth Bayley died, from mortification of the bowels, at Buxton, on 24th June, 1802, and was buried at Eccles, and in the parish church there is

[1] Baker's *Memorials.*
[2] *Monthly Repository*, 1814, p. 598.
[3] Canon Wray's *Memoirs*, p. 153.
[4] *Manchester Literary Club Papers*, v. 123.

the following inscription, probably written by Dr. Percival:—

> TO THE MEMORY OF THOMAS BUTTERWORTH BAYLEY, ESQ., OF HOPE HALL IN THIS PARISH. AN ACTIVE, INTELLIGENT, AND UPRIGHT MAGISTRATE, CANDID IN EXAMINATION, CLEAR IN JUDGMENT, FIRM IN DECISION, EVER TEMPERING JUSTICE WITH MERCY; A LIBERAL GUARDIAN AND INSTRUCTOR OF THE POOR; A ZEALOUS FRIEND; AN INTERESTING COMPANION; A HOSPITABLE NEIGHBOUR; A LOVER OF HIS COUNTRY AND MANKIND; AND A DEVOUT CHRISTIAN; THIS TABLET IS GRATE-FULLY AND AFFECTIONATELY INSCRIBED, BY HIS WIDOW AND CHILDREN. HE DIED JUNE 24TH, 1802, AGED 57 YEARS.
>
> MARY BAYLEY HIS WIDOW, LIES BURIED IN THE SAME VAULT BENEATH. SHE DIED AT THE FRIARY, LICHFIELD, SEPT. 5TH, 1818, AGED 70 YEARS.
>
> " THE HEART OF HER HUSBAND DID SAFELY TRUST IN HER,
> HER CHILDREN ROSE UP AND CALLED HER BLESSED,
> IN HER TONGUE WAS THE LAW OF KINDNESS,
> AND SHE STRETCHED OUT HER HAND TO THE POOR."

Thomas Butterworth Bayley married, at Tottenham Parish Church, 17th September, 1765, Mary, daughter of Vincent Leggatt, of Tottenham. By this lady he had issue:—

1. DANIEL (Sir), eldest son, born at Hope, 14th September, 1766, was educated at the Manchester Grammar School, which he entered 6th October, 1776, and at the Warrington Academy (admitted 1782). He became a merchant at St. Petersburg, being a partner in the great Russian house of Thorntons and Bayley (firm dissolved 30th April, 1810). He was appointed, 9th October, 1812. His Britannic Majesty's

Consul-General at St. Petersburg, and was also agent to the
Russia company.[1] He was knighted 20th June, 1815, and
his services as *chargé d'affaires*, during the absence of the
English ambassador, were also rewarded by the knighthood
of the Hanoverian Guelphic Order. Sir Daniel, some years
after his father's death, sold the Hope estate, and had hence-
forward little connection with his native county, but he was
a member of the Manchester Agricultural Society, and a
justice of the peace and deputy-lieutenant for the county
of Lancaster.[2] He died 21st June, 1834, and was bur. in
his máternal grandfather's grave at Tottenham.[3] Sir Daniel
Bayley was twice married, first at St. Petersburg, 6th
November, 1790, to Eleanor Saffree. She died at Hope, 13th
September, 1793, aged twenty-seven. Sir Daniel married
secondly, at St. Petersburg, 24th March, 1800, Maria Barbara
Fock, who died 19th May, 1854, aged seventy-nine, and was
bur. at Leamington, and by whom he had an only child:—

1. MARY, born at Hope, 22nd February, 1801: died at
   Leamington, 3rd May, 1878.

2. THOMAS LEGGATT, born 6th October, 1767; died 6th
September, 1768, at Hampstead, and was bur. at Tottenham.

3. THOMAS LEGGATT, born 1st April, 1769; died June,
1769, of smallpox by inoculation, and was bur. in the vault
at Hope.

4. SARAH, born 3rd August, 1770; died at Lichfield, where
she had resided over forty years, 28th July, 1845, and was
bur. at Elford, near Lichfield.

[1] "The consul's emoluments are superior to those in any other country.
I have heard them rated at 100,000 roubles per annum, including the
Hanoverian agency; this situation is held by Sir Daniel Bayley, Knt.,
which he obtained through the interest of Mr. Samuel Thornton, his late
partner in London. The society of these few families is limited to each
other; they have little intercourse with the Russians, and do not seem
forward in showing hospitality to strangers."—*Visit to St. Petersburg in
the Winter of* 1829-30, by Thomas Raikes, p. 182.

[2] *Manchester Courier,* 5th July, 1834.

[3] Cansick's *Epitaphs of Middlesex,* iii. 77.

5. HENRY CORNWALL, born 23rd January, 1772; died May, 1772, and was bur. at Hope.

6. MARY ANNE, born 21st April, 1774; died at Hampstead, 29th December, 1789, aged sixteen, and was bur. at Tottenham. To commemorate this young lady, John Aikin, M.D., wrote the following verses, which, with a portrait, were printed on a broadside:—[1]

TO THE MEMORY OF

### MARY ANNE BAYLEY,

WHO DIED DECEMBER 29TH, 1789. AGED SIXTEEN.

When loveliness array'd in opening Bloom,
   Framed to delight the Sense, the Heart to cheer,
Sinks early blasted to the silent Tomb,
   Who can suppress the Sigh, restrain the Tear?

Such was the Treasure lost, these lines record,
   And on the stone perused by kindred Eyes
Long shall that Name in faithful memory stored,
   Bid Sorrows flow, and keen Regrets arise.

But Faith sheds comfort on the troubled mind,
   And Gratitude recounts what once was given,
To Him who lent it be the Boon resigned!
   What soul too spotless, kind, and good for Heav'n?

7. JOHN, born at Hope, 19th May, 1775, educated at Winwick and at the Manchester Academy (commercial side), 1790-92.[2] He was apprenticed to Richard Wilson, cotton manufacturer. In 1794 he went to St. Petersburg, but returned in 1797. He died at Lichfield, 6th January, 1848, and was bur. at Elford.

8. EDWARD CLIVE, of whom presently.

9. HENRY VINCENT (Ven.), D.D., born at Hope, 6th December, 1777. He was educated at Winwick Grammar School and at Eton. In April, 1796, he commenced his

---

[1] A copy of the broadside is in the Binns Collection (vol. xvi., p. 54) in the Liverpool Free Library. See also *Manchester Guardian* "Notes and Queries," No. 1,054.
[2] Roll of Students, Manchester New College.

residence at Trinity College, Cambridge, and in 1800 took
the degree of B.A. and was first prizeman of the junior and
in the following year of the senior bachelors. He was then
pronounced by Porson to be the first Greek scholar of his
standing in England. In October, 1802, he was elected
fellow of his college, and became M.A. in the following year
and D.D. in 1824. He was ordained by Dr. Majendie,
bishop of Chester, whose chaplain he became. He shortly
afterwards became preceptor to Mr. W. E. Tomline, son of
the bishop of Lincoln, and received from the bishop the
rectory of Stilton, Huntingdonshire, 1804. In 1805 he was
appointed sub-dean of Lincoln, and prebend of Crackpool
St. Mary, in Lincoln Cathedral, and was installed 5th July,
1805. In 1806 he became vicar of Hibaldstow, Lincolnshire,
and in 1811 rector of Messingham with Bottesford. On
going to Lincoln Bayley found that one of the towers was
unsafe, and had it taken down; and, as the other tower was
now thought to be out of place, that also was removed. The
alterations caused considerable ill feeling towards the new
sub-dean. Mr. Bayley also had numerous monuments that
disfigured the walls of the cathedral removed, and placed in
a small chapel, thus restoring some of its pristine beauty to
the interior of the cathedral. Acting on Dr. Bayley's advice,
the Chapter sold, from the Cathedral Library, some Caxtons
to Dibdin for a very small sum, and with the proceeds purchased "more useful" books. Dr. Bayley established a joint-
stock library in Lincoln, and in 1813 founded some schools
on the Madras system. At Messingham he made numerous
improvements and alterations in the church. He purchased
from the Manchester Collegiate Church, then undergoing
extensive "improvements," some stained-glass windows,
which he placed in Messingham Church. In 1823 he became
archdeacon of Stow, and in 1826 rector of Westmeon with
Privet, Hampshire, resigning at the same time his living at
Messingham. Sunday was the favourite day of the Hampshire villagers for playing cricket, and this desecration of

the Lord's Day Dr. Bayley endeavoured in his own parish to
summarily put a stop to; but this aroused the anger of the
parishioners. He then tried other methods; he established a
Sunday afternoon service, but this only delayed Sunday
playing until a little later in the day, as the farm boys
brought their bats under their smocks and left them in the
porch during service, after which they proceeded to the
village green and began playing. Dr. Bayley then induced
the farmers to allow their labourers several hours on the week-
days for the game, and he had the satisfaction of thus having
abolished what, though Sunday recreation had been by no
means discouraged by the early English reformers, he considered to be a profanation of the Christian Sabbath. In
1828 he exchanged the sub-deanery of Lincoln for a canonry
of Westminster. He died 12th August, 1844, and was bur.
at Westmeon. The following passage from a MS. note by
Archdeacon Bonney, in a copy of Archdeacon Bayley's
"Charge," formerly in the possession of Mr. J. E. Bailey, is
worth quoting: "In person he [Dr. Bayley] was of the middle
size, inclining at one time to corpulency. His countenance
was full and expressive of benevolence; his manner good-
humoured, sprightly, and friendly, mixed often with a vein
of drollery which enlivened the spirits of his companion.
He was earnest in his religion without affectation, and a true
member of the Church of England, spending large sums out
of his own income in her cause, particularly towards refitting
of the church at Messingham and a new church in his parish
of Westmeon, which was nearly completed at the time of
his decease. In the last years of his life he became blind
and infirm, and died of natural decay without a pang or
sigh." Archdeacon Bayley married, at Eccles, 17th June,
1807, Hannah, second daughter of James Touchet, of Broom
House, to whom he was related, her grandmother having
been a daughter of James Bayley, senior. Mrs. Bayley
died, without issue, 17th June, 1839, and was bur. at
Westmeon.

10. FRANCES, born 5th March, 1779, and was bap. by
the Rev. Ralph Harrison, at her grandmother Bayley's house
in Manchester, April, 1779. She died at Leamington, 25th
December, 1840, and was bur. there.

11. CHARLES, born 13th March, 1780, and was bap. at
his grandmother's house in Manchester. He was appointed
a writer in the Bengal Civil Service in 1797. He was assistant to the secretary of the Board of Trade, 1798; assistant
to the commercial resident at Khairpur (Mr. Wilton, whose
niece he married), 1798; assistant to the salt agent at Tam-
luk, 1802, and commercial resident at Santipur, 1809. In
1811 he was appointed sub-export-warehouse-keeper and
reporter-general of external and internal commerce; in 1819
a junior member of the Board of Trade; in 1823, commercial
resident at Benares, Gorakhpur; in 1831, acting commercial
resident at Santipur. In 1833 he returned home and retired
from the Company's service in August, 1836.[1] He died at Cambridge Square, Hyde Park, on 19th January, 1865, and was
bur. at St. Leonards-on-Sea. Charles Bayley was married at
Calcutta, 30th March, 1800, to Mary Anne Smith, niece of
John Wilton, commercial resident at Khairpur (she died at
Richmond, 18th February, 1824, and was bur. at Chelsea Old
Church), and had issue:—

1. THOMAS WILTON, born at Calcutta, 9th January,
1802; died July, 1802, at Khairpur.

2. MARY ANNE, born at Calcutta, 22nd May, 1803,
and bap. at Eccles Church, 30th December, 1806,
with her two younger sisters. She died at sea, 6th
August, 1819.

3. HENRIETTA FRANCES, born 18th January, 1805;
married, 23rd March, 1824, to Edward Peploe Smith (a
great grandson of James Bayley, of Withington), and
died 18th December, 1824, leaving an only child, Mary
Anne, who died unmarried 1856.

---

[1] Dodwell and Miles's *Bengal Civil Servants.*

4. LUCY WILTON, born at Hope, 2nd October, 1806; died at Lichfield, 20th June, 1812, and was bur. at Elford, Staffordshire.

5. THOMAS BUTTERWORTH CHARLES, born at Calcutta, 21st November, 1810. Educated at the Charterhouse, which he entered in 1825. On 30th April, 1829, he was appointed a writer in Bengal Civil Service, and became, 24th May, 1831, assistant under the commissioner of Revenue, circuit 19th or Cuttack division, being transferred on 22nd November, 1831, to the 1st or Meerut division. He came home in 1836.[1] He died, unmarried, at Wynberg, Cape of Good Hope, 29th December, 1871.

6. WILTON REES, born at Calcutta, 6th March, 1812; educated at Charterhouse and Haileybury, and entered the Bengal Civil Service 30th April, 1830. In 1832 he was appointed assistant under the commissioner of Revenue, circuit 6 or Allahabad division. In the same year he returned home, and in 1837, having exceeded his five years' absence, left the Company's service.[2] He died in 1863, unmarried.

7. WILLIAM HENRY, born at Calcutta, 14th September, 1813. Entered the Madras Civil Service in 1831, and was in 1839 appointed deputy-secretary to Government under the chief secretary's department, and commissioner for drawing Government lotteries, and in 1843 commissioner in Karnul. In 1844 he came home on furlough, returning to India in 1848. In 1849 he was appointed sub-collector and joint magistrate of the Northern Division of Arcot; in 1850, secretary to the Board of Revenue, being reappointed in 1851 and 1855. In 1855 and 1856 he was third member of the Board of Revenue. In 1856 he was home on furlough, and returning to India

---

[1] Dodwell and Miles's *Bengal Civil Servants,* 1839.
[2] *Ibid.*

E

in 1857 was again third member of the Board of Revenue. In 1860 he came home on furlough, and in 1861 resigned the Company's service. He died at 5, Clarendon Terrace, Brighton, 20th August, 1890, in his seventy-seventh year, and was bur. in the Extra Mural Cemetery there. Mr. Bayley was the author of several works, of which a list is given in the appendix. Mr. Bayley married, at Trichinopoli, 9th April, 1836, Henrietta, daughter of William Young Ottley, F.R.S., F.S.A., custodian of the prints in the British Museum, and author of the *Italian School of Design*, &c. She died at Brighton, 13th November, 1876, and was bur. in the Extra Mural Cemetery. William Henry and Henrietta Bayley had issue:—

1. LUCY SEELY, born 4th February, 1837; living 1894.

2. HENRIETTA ELIZABETH, born 2nd January, 1838; married 14th November, 1865, the Rev. George Biscoe Oldfield, rector of Berwick St. Leonard-cum-Sedgehill, Wilts (youngest son of Henry Swann Oldfield of the Bengal Civil Service), and died 15th April, 1871, leaving issue: (1) Charles Bayley OLDFIELD, of New College, Oxford, and a barrister of the Inner Temple. (2) Gertrude Letitia. (3) Frederic Biscoe, of New College, Oxford, and a barrister of the Inner Temple.

3. ALICIA FENTON, born 30th March, 1839, and living 1894; married 9th December, 1869, James Robert Gaussen (second son of Charles Gaussen, of Dublin), who died 1870, leaving one child, Alice Ada Sophia, who died in 1872.

8. FREDERIC HAMILTON, born at Calcutta, 4th November, 1814; died 14th April, 1829, and was bur. at Fletching, Sussex.

12. WILLIAM BUTTERWORTH, of whom presently (Pedigree B).

13. CORNWALL, born 13th March, 1784, and was bap. at Hope, 19th April, 1784, by the Rev. Thomas Barnes, D.D. He was educated at Winwick and Rugby, and on 7th December, 1801, was entered at Christ's College, Cambridge. In April, 1804, he went to America, and returned to England, October, 1806. He died of consumption, November, 1807, at Doncaster, and was bur. there. While in America he had, on 18th May, 1806, married Helen Eliza Jones, who died at Ballymena, County Antrim, in 1809, leaving one child:—

> 1. MARY, born at York, 3rd April, 1807, and died at Ballymena, November, 1846, having married, in 1836, Captain Richard Dyas. Captain and Mrs. Dyas had issue: Richard Hudson, James Jones, and a daughter, who died in infancy.

14. FREDERICK, born at Hope, 29th May, 1785. He died November, 1785, and was bur. at Hope, 29th November, 1785.

15. THOMAS DUKINFIELD, born 3rd March, 1787, and was bap. at Hope by Rev. R. Harrison, 10th April, 1787. He was educated at Winwick and Rugby. He was in the Russia trade, but was drowned at sea, off Memel, 7th April, 1808, having been washed overboard from the "Agatha," in which he was returning to Russia.

16. A daughter, born 28th September, 1789, and died immediately.

17. GEORGE THORNTON, born at Hope, 3rd December, 1790, and was bap. there by the curate of Eccles. He was educated at Rugby, the Charterhouse, and Haileybury. In 1807 he became a writer in the Bengal Civil Service, and was register to the Zillah Court of Hugli, 1812; register to the Court of Appeal at Calcutta, 1814; assistant in the office of the secretary in the Revenue and Judicial department in 1815,

and acting register and joint magistrate of suburbs of Calcutta in 1816. At the end of that year he went home and returned to India in 1821. In 1822 he was appointed collector of Shahabad; in 1826 deputy opium agent at Shahabad; in 1828, collector of land revenue and deputy collector of Government customs and town duties, and deputy opium agent at Gházipur. In 1833 he returned home, and on 31st May, 1835, died at Devonshire Place, London. He was bur. at Tottenham.

## VI.

EDWARD CLIVE BAYLEY, born 16th August, 1776, and educated at the Manchester Academy, 1790-92.[1] He was for many years a successful merchant at St. Petersburg, where he died 23rd February, 1841, and was buried with his wife and his children, Mary Margaret, and Thomas, in the Protestant burial ground of Smolensk, St. Petersburg. He married at Cheltenham, 2nd July, 1814,[2] Margaret, eldest daughter of James Fenton, of Hampstead, by whom he had issue six children, who were all born at St. Petersburg:—

1. MARY MARGARET, born June, 1815; died there 14th September (O.S.), 26th September (N.S.), 1821.
2. ELIZABETH CATHCART, born 1st September, 1816.
3. ELEANOR LOUISA, born 3rd October, 1817.
4. THOMAS BUTTERWORTH, born June, 1819; died at St. Petersburg, 15th July, 1819 (O.S.).
5. FRANCES CUMMING, born June, 1820.
6. EDWARD CLIVE, of whom presently.

[1] Roll of Students, Manchester New College.
[2] Exchange Herald, 12th July, 1814.

## VII.

SIR EDWARD CLIVE BAYLEY, K.C.S.I., C.I.E., only surviving son of Edward Clive Bayley, was born at St. Petersburg, 17th October, 1821, and, after having distinguished himself at Haileybury, entered the Bengal Civil Service in 1842. He commenced his official career at Allahabad, and subsequently held appointments at Meerut, Bulandshahr, and Rohtak. On the annexation of the Panjab, he was appointed a deputy-commissioner, and entered on his duties at Gujârât in 1849. In the same year he became under-secretary to the Government of India in the Foreign Department. In 1851 he was appointed deputy-commissioner of the Kangra district of the Punjab, but in 1854 ill-health compelled him to take furlough in England. He was called to the Bar in 1857, and, shortly after the outbreak of the Mutiny, returned to India, and was ordered in September, 1857, to Allahabad, where he acted as one of the under-secretaries in Sir John P. Grant's provisional government, and afterwards as magistrate at Allahabad. In 1859 he was appointed judge in the Futtehgurh district, and afterwards was judicial commissioner at Lucknow, and judge at Agra. For a short time he acted as foreign secretary to the Government of India, and in March, 1862, became home secretary. This post he filled until 1872, when he was appointed to a temporary vacancy in the council. In the following year he became an ordinary member of the Supreme Council, which post he filled until his retirement from the civil service in April, 1878. He was created a K.C.S.I. on January 1st, 1877. During his long career in India, Sir E. Clive Bayley was a devoted friend of the natives, and in all the different posts he held their welfare was his chief object. During his leisure hours he studied deeply the history of the people: their traditions, their literature, their arts, and their archæology, and became the chief authority on the numismatic history of India. Sir Edward Clive Bayley was five times elected president of the Bengal Asiatic Society, and was for five years vice-chancellor of the University of Calcutta. Sir Clive Bayley died at Wilmington Lodge, Keymer, on the 30th April, 1884.

A list of Sir Clive Bayley's writings, together with a lengthy biography, appears in the Annual Report for 1884 of the Royal Asiatic Society, of which he was a vice-president.

Sir Edward Clive Bayley married at Delhi, 6th March, 1850, Emily Anne Theophilia, eldest daughter of Sir Thomas Theophilus Metcalfe, baronet, H.E.I.C.S., by his second wife, Felicite Anne, eldest daughter of John Browne, of the Bengal Medical Board. Lady Bayley is a niece of Charles Lord Metcalfe, G.C.B., Governor-General of Canada. Sir Edward Clive and Lady Bayley had issue:—

1. EMILY ISABELLA CLIVE, born at Simla, December, 1850; married 8th March, 1883, at Savoy Chapel, London, to George Henry Mildmay Ricketts, C.B., and has issue, Edward Wallace Claud, born 1st April, 1884.

2. ANNIE MARGARET CLIVE, born at Nagpur, March, 1852.

3. EDWARD METCALFE CLIVE, born at North Stoneham, Hants, 16th August, 1854; died in London, January, 1859, and was bur. at North Stoneham.

4. GEORGIANA CHARLOTTE CLIVE, born in London, December, 1855; married 3rd December, 1886, at Ascot, to Major-General Edward Francis Chapman, C.B.

5. ALICE JANET CLIVE, born in London, December, 1856; married 14th December, 1878, at St. George's, Hanover Square, to John Arthur Fowler, eldest son of Sir John Fowler, Bart., K.C.M.G., and has issue: Mabel Elizabeth, born 1882; Marjorie Theophila, born 1884; John Edward, born 1885, and Alan Arthur, born 1887.

6. MABEL ELLIOTT CLIVE, born in London, April, 1858; died at Eastbourne, November, 1877, and was bur. there.

7. MARY THEOPHILA STEUART CLIVE, born at Lucknow, August, 1860.

8. CHARLOTTE ANSTRUTHER CANNING CLIVE, born at Calcutta, November, 1861.

9. CHARLES THEOPHILUS RICHARD CLIVE, of whom presently.

10. THERESA SELINA CLIVE, born at Simla, June, 1866.

11. KATE SAINTON CLIVE, born at Simla, July, 1867, and died there 11th June, 1869.

## VIII.

CHARLES THEOPHILUS RICHARD CLIVE BAYLEY, born at Simla, 20th November, 1864. Mr. Charles T. R. C. Bayley is the present head of the family and is treasurer to the Niger Protectorate.

## B.—WILLIAM BUTTERWORTH BAYLEY AND HIS DESCENDANTS.

### VI.

WILLIAM BUTTERWORTH BAYLEY (twelfth child of Thomas Butterworth Bayley, F.R.S.), born 3rd November, 1781, and baptized at his grandmother's house in Manchester, 7th January, 1782. He was educated at Winwick and Eton, and went to Trinity College, Cambridge 1798. On 18th June, 1799, he sailed for Bengal, having obtained an appointment in the Bengal Civil Service; and, on reaching India, was entered as a member of the new College of Fort William, which Lord Wellesley had just established for the education of the Indian civil servants. Of the College of Fort William Mr. Bayley was one of the most distinguished alumni. In 1800 he took a second prize in the third class for Hindustani, and in 1802 proved his talent for languages by being in the first class in Persian. On completing his college course he was selected by the Governor-General for the confidential duties of his own office. Here, in company with Metcalfe and others of the cleverest of the young civil servants, Mr. Bayley learned the art of government under Lord Wellesley's eye. He decided to confine himself to the routine of judicial and revenue work. In 1805 he was made deputy-registrar of the Sudder Court, and in 1807 interpreter to the commission for regulating the government and land settlement of the North-Western Provinces. In 1809 he was appointed judge at Dacca Jalalpur; in 1810, judge at Bardwan; and, in 1814, fourth judge of the Provincial Court of Appeal, first at Bareilly and then at Dacca. In 1814 he entered the secretariat as secretary to the Revenue and Judicial departments, and in 1819 became chief secretary to the Government, in which capacity he was of the greatest service to Lord Hastings. In 1822 he temporarily filled a seat at the council, and in 1825 became a regular member of the Supreme Council. In 1828 he filled the office of governor-general of India from March 13th to 4th July, when he became president of the Board of Trade. He returned to England April, 1831, and retired from the Company's service 1st May, 1834. Mr. Bayley was elected a director of the East India Company 23rd July, 1833, and remained a director until 1854, in which year he declined nomination as a permanent director. He was deputy-chairman in 1839, and chairman of the court in 1840. Mr. W. B. Bayley died at St. Leonards-on-Sea, 20th May, 1860. Mr. Bayley's work, though perhaps not so conspicuous as that of his contemporaries, Lord Metcalfe or Jenkins, was no less important, and it was due entirely to his unobtrusive modesty that he received no titular distinction or reward for his services.

William Butterworth Bayley, married, February, 1809, at Calcutta, Anne Augusta, daughter of William Jackson, registrar of the Supreme Court, Calcutta, and solicitor to the Hon. East India Company. She was born January, 1792, and died at Bath, 19th April, 1848, aged fifty-six, having had:—

    1. HENRY VINCENT, of whom presently.

    2. HARRIET STEUART, born December, 1817, and died June, 1819.

F

3. MARY STEUART, born November, 1820; married 29th February, 1840, at St. George's, Hanover Square, to Bazett David Colvin, J.P., and had with other issue, who died in infancy, WILLIAM (died 1883), lieut.-colonel, commanding 21st Fusiliers, and SIDNEY, M.A., professor of fine arts at Cambridge, and keeper of the department of prints in the British Museum.

4. DANIEL, born 26th August, 1822. In the military service of the East India Company from 1839 to 1854, when he retired with the rank of captain. Captain Bayley married at Brighton, 30th August, 1849, Isabella Frances, daughter of William Henry Oakes, B.C.S., and widow of David Scott Carmichael Smyth, B.C.S., and had issue:—

1. ISABELLA TEMPE, born in India, 1851; died at Florence, 29th November, 1853.

2. CHARLES STUART, born at Florence, March, 1854. Educated at Harrow and Heidelberg. Called to the Bar, Lincoln's Inn, 1877. Entered the Bengal Civil Service, 1875; arrived in India in 1877. Has been under-secretary to the Government of India revenue and agricultural department, and is now political agent at Bikanir.

Charles Stuart Bayley, married at Sibsagar, Assam, 18th December, 1880, Sarah Constance, second daughter of Major-General Archibald Edwardes Campbell, of the Indian Staff Corps, and has had the following children:—

1. ISABEL CONSTANCE, born 2nd November, 1881: died 24th June, 1882.

2. FLORENCE TEMPE, born 26th October, 1883.

3. ARCHIBALD STEUART BUTTERWORTH, born 8th July, 1885.

4. ETHEL HERMIONE, born 11th July, 1888.

5. ALICE MARY, born 8th November, 1891.

5. WILLIAM BUTTERWORTH MASTER, born October, 1827, and died June, 1879.

6. HENRIETTA FRANCES, born in London March, 1832, married 4th September, 1856, at St. Peter's, Eaton Square, to

John Scarlett Campbell, B.C.S., and died October, 1859, at Futtehgurh, having had issue: William, born and died in 1857, and Lilian, born 1858, married Martin Henry Pirie, and has issue: Harold Victor Campbell, born 1884, and Wilfrid Bayley, born 1887.

7. EDWARD HENRY, born in London, 25th June, 1834. Educated at Eton and at Christ's College, Cambridge; B.A. 1858, M.A. 1861. Was intended for holy orders, but ill-health prevented him following any profession. He married, 10th September, 1862, Amelia Maria, third daughter of Edward Emmet, of Halifax, and died at Southport, 23rd February, 1893, having had an only child :—

> AMY STEUART, born 4th June, 1863, and married, 10th September, 1885, to James Alfred Harris, M.D. (Lond.), of Chorley, J.P. for Lancashire.

8. STEUART COLVIN (Sir), born 26th November, 1836. Having been educated at Eton and Haileybury, he entered the Bengal Civil Service, arrived at India in 1856. His principal appointments were junior secretary to the Government of Bengal in 1863, commissioner of the Patna division in 1873, personal assistant to the Viceroy for famine affairs in 1877, chief commissioner of Assam in 1878, resident at Hyderabad in 1881, member of the Governor-General's Council in 1882, and lieutenant-governor of Bengal in 1887. Sir Steuart's present post is that of secretary, political and secret department, India Office, which he has held since January, 1891. He received the C.S.I. in 1874, the K.C.S.I. in 1878, and the C.I.E. in 1882. Sir Steuart married at Patna, 21st November, 1860, Anna, daughter of Robert Nesham Farquharson, B.C.S., and has had issue:—

> 1. CLIVE WILLIAM, born at Arrah, 10th September, 1862; died, from an accident, at Calcutta, November, 1863.

> 2. STEUART FARQUHARSON, born at Burhanpur, 14th August, 1863. Is a lieutenant in the Bengal Staff Corps.

3. FRANCES MARY LUSHINGTON, born at Calcutta, February, 1865; died at sea, near Madras, 12th April, 1865.

4. ETHEL AUGUSTA COLVIN, born at Calcutta, 9th May, 1867; married at St. Paul's Cathedral, Calcutta, 7th December, 1889, to Elliot Graham Colvin, B.C.S.

5. WILLIAM EDEN, born at Patna, 6th June, 1869, and educated at Winchester.

6. ALICIA SIDNEY, born at Muzafferpur, 4th October, 1870; married 2nd December, 1890, to William Buckley Gladstone, of Calcutta.

7. MARION HAMILTON, born 11th March, 1873.

8. CLIVE CAMPBELL, born 22nd March, 1874, and died 23rd April, 1876.

9. LIONEL SETON, born in London, 2nd July, 1875.

10. CHARLES BUTTERWORTH, born in London, 7th September, 1876.

11. LYTTON CECIL LAMBERT, born at Shillong, Assam, 9th April, 1879.

12. MELVILL GORDON, born at Bolaram, Deccan, 7th March, 1885.

13. NORAH LILIAN, born at Simla, 22nd March, 1886; died 27th May, 1886.

## VII.

HENRY VINCENT BAYLEY (eldest son of William Butterworth Bayley) was born on 27th July, 1816, and was educated at Eton and Haileybury. He became a writer in the Bengal Civil Service in April, 1835, and after having held various positions of importance, became, 13th May, 1862, judge of the High Court of Judicature, Calcutta, and retained that post until his death, which occurred at Calcutta, 2nd February, 1873.

Henry Vincent Bayley married at Calcutta, 6th

December, 1838, Louisa, daughter of James Pattle, B.C.S. (she was born 5th October, 1821, and died in London, March, 1873), and had issue:—

1. ADELINE ANNE, born 22nd October, 1842, married at Barrackpur, Calcutta, 21st April, 1863, to William F. Mactier, M.D., and has had issue:—

(1) ADELINE, born 1864; died 1864. (2) WILLIAM BUTTERWORTH, M.B., of Liverpool, born 1865. (3) HENRY MACKINNON, born 1866. (4) ANTHONY DOUGLAS, born 1867. (5) MARIA LOUISA, born 1867; died 1878. (6) ADELINE HARRIS, born 1871. (7) CHARLES BAYLEY, born 1873. (8) THOMAS BINNEY, born 1875; died 1880. (9) MINNIE MOIR, born 1882.

2. MIA LOUISA, born 25th September, 1845, married at Calcutta, 6th March, 1865, to Nottidge Charles Macnamara, F.R.C.S., and has issue:—

(1) NORA, born 1866; married, 1888, to Montagu Lubbock, M.D., of Grosvenor Street, London. (2) ADELINE LOUISA, born 1867; married, 1893, to Captain Hubert Rouse, R.A. (3) OONA, born 1870; married, 1890, to Bertram Prior Standen, B.C.S. (4) CHARLES CAROLL, born 1875. (5) SHEILA, born 1876. (6) MAIVE, born 1879. (7) DOROTHY MIA, born 1882. (8) PATRICK GUY, born 1886.

3. WILLIAM DE L'ETANG, born at Brighton, 17th January, 1849, and died at The Priory, Hampstead, 28th September, 1867.

4. HENRY, born 4th May, 1852; educated at Rugby and Trinity College, Oxford. He was in the Bengal Police, and died in India, June, 1879. He married in 1878, Ariana Le Marchand, and had an only child:—

MAY, born May, 1879.

## C.—BAYLEY OF WITHINGTON.

### IV.

JAMES BAYLEY, of Withington (third son of James Bayley, the elder, of Manchester), was born 24th March, 1705. In early life he was a merchant in Manchester, and was one of the constables of the town in 1735. On the 9th August, 1745, he was constituted, by his father-in-law, Bishop Peploe, registrar of the diocese of Chester. In 1757 he was high sheriff of Lancashire, and about the same period became an active justice of the peace. He was approved a deputy-lieutenant of the county, 27th April, 1761.[1] At his death, 14th November, 1769, it was said that "in him were united the good Christian, the affectionate husband, the tender parent, and the sincere friend."[2] He was buried in the Collegiate Church, Manchester. He married, 31st January, 1727, Anne, daughter of the Right Rev. Samuel Peploe, D.D., bishop of Chester and warden of Manchester. She was baptized at Preston in November, 1702, and died 29th November, 1769, having survived her husband only a fortnight. James and Anne Bayley had issue:—

1. SARAH, born 16th and bap. 30th November, 1728, at the Collegiate Church. She was married in 1754 to Dorning Rasbotham, J.P., high sheriff of Lancashire in 1769, and for twenty years chairman of quarter sessions, and died 30th April, 1805, aged seventy-seven.

---

[1] Rawstorne's *Royal Lancashire Militia*, p. 119.
[2] Harrop's *Manchester Mercury*.

2. ANNE, bap. 29th January, 1729-30, at St. Anne's, Manchester; married at Northenden,[1] 18th April, 1750, the Ven. Abel Ward, M.A., rector of St. Anne's, Manchester, and archdeacon of Chester. She was bur. at Chester Cathedral, 20th December, 1806.

3. MARY, born 6th December, 1730; bap. at the Collegiate Church, 28th January, 1730-1, and died unmarried.

4. ELIZABETH, bap. at the Collegiate Church, 7th March, 1731-2.

5. SAMUEL, bap. at St. Anne's, 2nd February, 1732-3. Educated at the Manchester Grammar School and was an officer in the Army. He married Miss Wall, of Colchester, and had an only child:—

    1. ANNE.

6. MARY, bap. 9th May, 1734; bur. at St. Anne's.

7. ELIZABETH, bap. at St. Anne's, 3rd December, 1735; married at the Collegiate Church, 7th April, 1760, to Sir John Parker Mosley, baronet, and died 15th October, 1797. From this marriage are descended the families of Mosley, of Rolleston, Feilden, Every, Master, and others.

8. JAMES, bap. 5th July, 1737, at St. Anne's. Died in infancy.

9. JAMES (Rev.), of whom presently.

10. JOHN, bap. 31st March, 1741. He was educated at the Manchester Grammar School and was a check manufacturer in Manchester. To him his brother James, by his will, dated 15th December, 1792, left the whole of his estate, after the death of his wife, "on account of his many infirmities;" but by a codicil, two days later, he directed that his brother was "to take only with his sisters, as he has sunk his property, and has a considerable annuity thereby." John Bayley died unmarried.

11. JANE, bap. 5th July, 1743, at St. Anne's, and was married

---

[1] Earwaker's *East Cheshire*, i. 305.

to the Rev. Thomas Walker, rector of Standon, Staffordshire, and left one son.

12. APPYLINA or APPOLONIA, bap. 18th September, 1744, at St. Anne's. Her Christian name of Appolonia she derived from her maternal grandmother's family, the Brownes, of Shredicote, members of the family having for several generations borne it. She married first, on 7th January, 1765, James Moss, of Manchester, lord of the manor of Little Bolton. He died in 1769. She married, secondly, at the Collegiate Church, Manchester, 4th February, 1772, the Rev. Giles Fairclough Haddon, D.D., rector of Stepney, and died on the 1st April, 1773.

13. FRANCES, bap. 14th August, 1746, at St. Anne's, and married at Prestwich, 23rd December, 1764, to Sir Ashton Lever, knight, of Alkrington, F.R.S., collector of the Leverian Museum. Lady Lever was bur. at Prestwich, 27th July, 1802.

14. ARABELLA, bap. 29th September, 1747, at St. Anne's; bur. at St. Anne's, 16th July, 1748.

## V.

Rev. JAMES BAYLEY. Baptized 28th February, 1740, at St. Anne's, Manchester, and educated at the Manchester Grammar School. He matriculated at Oxford (Brazenose College), 23rd February, 1759; was a Hulmean Exhibitioner 1762, B.A. 1762, and M.A. 1765. In 1764 he became rector of St. Mary's, Manchester, in 1765 one of the chaplains and in 1773 a fellow of the Collegiate Church, Manchester. He is described by those who knew him as a very courteous man, with great social and personal accomplishments. He suffered much from gout and rheumatism, and was lame for several years before he died. The Rev. James Bayley died 13th November,

1808, and was buried at the Collegiate Church. He married at the Collegiate Church, 12th February, 1771, Frances, daughter and coheiress of Richard Broome, of Mile End, near Didsbury, and of Manchester, attorney-at-law. She was baptized at St. Anne's 27th June, 1744, and died 6th June, 1818, and was buried with her husband.[1]  The Rev. James Bayley had no children.

---

[1] Some further particulars of the Rev. James Bayley and of his wife will be found in Raines's *Lives of the Fellows of the College of Manchester*, edited by Dr. Renaud, p. 287.

## D.—BAYLEY OF BOOTH HALL.

### IV.

SAMUEL BAYLEY, of King Street, Manchester (son of James Bayley, senior), was born 31st December, 1717, and was a linen draper and check manufacturer. He was appointed a trustee of Cross Street Chapel in 1746, and died 5th March, 1778, aged sixty years, and was buried at Cross Street.[1] He married first, at Blackley Chapel, 1741, Esther, daughter of James Diggles, of Manchester, merchant, and niece and, in her issue, heiress of Thomas Diggles, of Booth Hall, Blackley. Esther Diggles received, under the will (proved 1732) of her father, the sum of £2,000. She died 12th September, 1758, and was buried with her husband at Cross Street. Samuel Bayley married, secondly, at the Collegiate Church, 28th April, 1761,[2] Esther, daughter of Robert Hibbert, of Manchester, merchant, and of Stockfield House, Oldham. She died 27th December, 1772, aged fifty-eight, and was buried at St. Anne's,[3] having had no issue.

The children of Samuel Bayley by his first marriage were :—

1. HANNAH, legatee of £1,000 under the will of her uncle, Thomas Diggles, 1771, and of £5,000 under that of John Diggles, 1782, married William Edge, of Manchester, merchant.

2. JAMES, died March, 1745, aged one; bur. at Cross Street.[4]

---

[1] Baker's *Memorials*, p. 84.        [2] John Owen's *MSS.*
[3] *Manchester City News* Notes and Queries, 1885.
[4] John Owen's *MSS.*

3. John, died October, aged one; bur. at Cross Street.[1]

4. Thomas, of whom presently.

5. Sarah, legatee of £1,000 under her uncle's, Thomas Diggles, will, and of £5,000 under that of John Diggles, married at the Collegiate Church, in December, 1773, to Cornelius Metcalfe, of Manchester, and afterwards of London, wine merchant.[2] Mr. and Mrs. Metcalfe resided in France from 1791 to 1795. In 1793, they and their three daughters were arrested and imprisoned at Rouen, under a decree by which all British subjects in France were imprisoned and their property confiscated.[3] Cornelius and Sarah Metcalfe had issue, with four daughters, an only son, whose descendants have been intimately connected with India.

6. James, of whom presently (Pedigree E).

## V.

Thomas Bayley, of Booth Hall and of Manchester, merchant. Under the will of his maternal uncle, John Diggles, Mr. Bayley became possessed of Booth Hall, Blackley, with other estates in Blackley and Droylsden. He was a trustee, from 1778 to 1817, of Cross Street Chapel, and for several years chapel treasurer. He died 22nd November, 1817, aged sixty-eight.[1] His will, dated 15th January, 1816, is printed in Booker's *Blackley*. He married, at the Collegiate Church, 18th November, 1773, Mary, daughter of William Kennedy, of Manchester, fustian manufacturer. She died 11th January, 1808, having had issue:—

1. Samuel, bap. 23rd August, 1774. He was a merchant in Manchester, and afterwards a member of the London Stock Exchange. He was ensign of the Manchester and

---

[1] John Owen's *MSS*.          [3] Foster's *Yorkshire Pedigrees*.
[2] Whitaker's *Craven*.          [1] Baker's *Memorials*, p. 89.

Salford Volunteers 1797, and was appointed captain Second Supplementary Militia, co. Lanc., 16th February, 1797.[1] He was a trustee of Cross Street Chapel from 1802 until his death. He died of jaundice at 44, Southernhay, Exeter, 25th July, 1854.

2. MARY, born 25th November, 1775; married 27th June, 1803, at the Collegiate Church, to William Henry, M.D., F.R.S., of Manchester, who purchased the Booth Hall estate in 1818, and shortly afterwards sold it. She died at Haffield, Ledbury, 25th November, 1837, having had issue William Charles Henry, M.D., F.R.S., J.P. co. Hereford, who died 1892; and Lucy, wife of William Rathbone Greg.

3. ESTHER, born 1st March, 1777. During a visit to Edinburgh she became acquainted with Robert Burns. On the 24th September, 1812, she was married at the Collegiate Church to Thomas Potter, merchant, afterwards first mayor of Manchester and a knight, by whom she had two sons, Sir John Potter, M.P., and Thomas Bayley Potter, M.P. Lady Potter was a worthy assistant of Sir Thomas Potter in his many philanthropic schemes, and was the founder in 1818 of Lady Potter's schools at Irlams-o'th'-Height, which she supported until her death. She died 19th June, 1852.

4. WILLIAM KENNEDY, see below.

5. JOHN DIGGLES, born in 1781. He was a merchant in Manchester, and on 6th September, 1803, became captain of the St. George's battalion of the Manchester Volunteers.[2] He died in 1848.

6. SARAH, born in 1783; died at Wimbledon, 27th July, 1868.

7. THOMAS DIGGLES, born in 1784. Entered the army and served at Walcheran. He became a lieutenant in the Fifty-sixth Foot, 25th December, 1813. After his retirement on half-pay in 1814, he resided at Ramsgate, where he was master of ceremonies at the public balls, a post for which his

---

[1] Rawsthorne's *Royal Lancashire Militia*, pp. 18, 20.
[2] *Local Gleanings*, ii. 212.

handsome appearance and military training well fitted him. He died in London unmarried on 30th April, 1831.

8. GILBERT, born 1786, and died 1810.

9. ELIZABETH, born 1787. Miss Eliza Bayley received from her maternal aunt, Mrs. Robert Riddell, a copy of the *Scots Musical Museum*, containing many annotations in the handwriting of Robert Burns, which Miss Bayley gave Cromek permission to publish. She died at East Hill House, Hastings, 29th August, 1846.

10. ANNE, born 1789; died at Bath 15th September, 1859.

11. ROBERT RIDDELL, born 1791. Was of Basinghall Street, and of Mitchett Lodge, Frimley, Surrey, and died 29th February, 1852.

## VI.

WILLIAM KENNEDY BAYLEY, born 1778. He was a student at the Manchester Academy from 1794 to 1796, and afterwards went to Jamaica, where he died in 1806. He married at Liverpool, 19th January, 1803, Isabel, daughter of John Russell, of Clarendon, Jamaica, and had issue:—

WILLIAM KENNEDY, born in Jamaica. Barrister-at-law, Lincoln's Inn. He was killed whilst alighting from a train at St. Pancras Station, *circa* 1867.

# E.—JAMES BAYLEY, OF BROWN STREET, AND HIS DESCENDANTS.

## V.

JAMES BAYLEY, of Brown Street, Manchester (son of Samuel Bayley and Esther Diggles), was born in 1757, and was educated at the Warrington Academy. He became a cotton merchant in Manchester, being head of the firm of James Bayley and Son, which dissolved partnership in 1804. James Bayley received £1,000 under the will (1771) of his great uncle, Thomas Diggles, and by the will (1781) of his uncle, John Diggles, the testator's houses and lands in Cateaton Street and Millbrow, Manchester. Mr. Bayley was a prominent dissenter, and a trustee of Cross Street Chapel from 1782 until his death. He was a member of the first committee for the establishment of the Manchester Academy, now the Manchester College, Oxford. At the Manchester assemblies, held in his later years, Mr. Bayley acted as master of the ceremonies, and exercised an autocratic rule over the guests. He was a fine old gentleman, and on these occasions was always powdered and carried under his arm a *chapeau de bras*.[1] Towards the end of his life Mr. Bayley lived at Southport, and died there in 1842.[2] James Bayley married, at the Collegiate Church, 3rd June, 1776, Margaret, daughter

---

[1] *Manchester Guardian*, February 18th, 1882.
[2] His portrait is in the possession of Mr. Francis S. Bayley, of Fallowfield.

of James Hodson, of Manchester. check manufacturer. She was born 10th January, 1756, and was educated at Miss Chalmers' boarding school, Liverpool. A little manuscript volume, written by Miss Hodson while she was at school, is in the possession of her great grandson. Mr. Francis S. Bayley, of Fallowfield. It contains, besides extracts from favourite authors, a number of original poems of considerable merit for so young a writer. One of the poems, Miss Hodson states, was written "at the request of my intimate schoolfellows, on favourite gentlemen that we were well acquainted with, and whom we called by flowers to deceive our sister nuns and abbesses." Mrs. Bayley died 18th June, 1793, aged thirty-seven, and was buried at Cross Street Chapel. James and Margaret Bayley had issue :—

1. JAMES DIGGLES, born 10th February, 1778; died 16th December, 1779.

2. SAMUEL, of whom presently.

3. MARGARET, born 16th January, 1782; died January, 1825, and was bur. at Cross Street.

4. JAMES, born 5th July, 1783. He entered the military service of the East India Company, Madras Presidency, as a cadet, in 1802; became lieutenant, 21st September, 1804; captain, 18th October, 1819; and major, 21st June, 1827. He retired 4th July, 1829, and died in 1846. Major Bayley was twice married, but left no children.

5. FRANCES, born 22nd July, 1784. She was married, first, to John Barlow, of Middlethorpe, Yorkshire; and, secondly, to Captain Hamilton.

6. DIGGLES, born 22nd March, 1787 (? of Cape Coast Castle. His widow, Harriet, married 3rd August, 1831, Lieutenant E. G. Palmer, R.N.[1])

---

[1] *Gentleman's Magazine*, August, 1831, p. 171.

7. AMY ANN, born 1791; died 1882, and was bur. at Southport.

## VI.

SAMUEL BAYLEY (called "the younger," to distinguish him from his cousin of the same name), of Didsbury. Born 16th March, 1779, and was educated at the Manchester Academy. He was a cotton merchant in Manchester in business with his father, and was afterwards a member of the banking house of Daintry, Ryle, and Co., and managing partner of that firm's Manchester bank. He retired in 1833. Mr. Bayley was a trustee of Cross Street Chapel under the trusts of 1802, 1809, 1821, and 1828. He died at the Avenue, Ellesmere, Shropshire, 9th September, 1857.[1]

Samuel Bayley married Harriet Anne, daughter of Richard Walker, of Manchester. She died at Aylesmore, Hewelsfield, 28th April, 1846, aged sixty-three.

Samuel and Harriet Anne Bayley had issue:—

1. JAMES WALKER, of whom presently.
2. SAMUEL HENRY, married and had issue a son, Henry.
3. HARRIET PARR, living unmarried at Southport (1894).
4. FRANCIS, of Apsley Cottage, Ardwick, and King

---

[1] Mr. Samuel Bayley was the victim of an audacious highway robbery. The *Gentleman's Magazine* for 1813, p. 175, gives this account of the circumstance: "Feb. 6.—Between seven and eight o'clock, as Mr. Samuel Bayley, cotton merchant, was riding towards home, on the Rusholme Road, he was suddenly entangled by a rope, stretched across the road, for the purpose of robbery. His mare was upon a short canter, and he was in a moment swept off her back, and instantly seized by four men, who told him if he made any resistance they would shoot him. They proceeded to rifle him of his property, and told him to proceed and make no alarm, or his life should pay for it. He endeavoured in vain to recover his mare, but she found her way home alone, about six o'clock next morning."

Street, Manchester, sharebroker and agent  Born in 1808. Died 27th September, 1839, and was bur. at Didsbury. Francis Bayley married, at the Collegiate Church, 24th September, 1836, Mary Ann, youngest daughter of John Taylor, of Mosley Street, Manchester, solicitor. She died 22nd April, 1884, aged seventy-four, and was bur. with her husband. Francis and Mary Ann Bayley had issue:—

    1. MARY LOUISA, born 28th June, 1837, and was married to Hervey Kibble.

    2. FRANCIS SAMUEL, of Norton House, Fallowfield, and of King Street, Manchester, chemical merchant, born 18th September, 1838. He married, in 1866, Mary Elizabeth Jane, eldest daughter of John Thomas Price, J.P., of Rusholme, and has issue:—

        1. FRANCIS PRICE, born 22nd February, 1867.

        2. MARY AMY, born 8th October, 1868.

        3. ELLEN, born 9th November, 1869, and was married, in 1891, to Henry Elton.

        4. KATHARINE, born 27th May, 1871.

        5. JOHN PARR, born 4th July, 1873.

        6. GEORGE ANSON, born 16th July, 1875.

        7. ARCHIBALD, born 1st February, 1877.

        8. CLIVE CHRISTIAN, born 25th December, 1878, and died 12th February, 1879.

        9. HUGH, born 22nd July, 1880.

        10. CHARLES SEPTIMUS, born 21st March, 1882.

    3. ADELAIDE FRANCES, born 23rd October, 1839, and was married to William Railton.

## VII.

JAMES WALKER BAYLEY entered the Madras army in 1819, and served in the Coorg campaign of 1834 and in the campaign of 1844-5 in the southern Mahratta country. He became a major-general in 1867, and died 30th November, 1874. Major-General Bayley married,

H

first, Annabella Maxwell Crawfurd: and, secondly, Mary Ann Phelan; and had issue, by his first wife:—

1. FRANCES RALSTON, married to Lieut.-General David Shaw, Madras Staff Corps, and died in 1893.

2. JAMES CRAWFURD, born 3rd December, 1833, lieutenant, Madras Staff Corps. Married, and had issue:—

> JAMES REGINALD, born 30th June, 1890, and died 19th February, 1892;

and by his second wife:—

3. MARY, married to Colonel Johnson, Madras Staff Corps.

4. KATE, married to Frank Bigg-Wither, Madras Native Infantry, medical staff.

5. WILLIAM CLEMENTS, major, Madras Staff Corps. He married Janie, daughter of — Murray, LL.D., of Dublin, and died in India.

6. HENRY ELLIOTT DASHWOOD, born 27th May, 1840; entered the Madras Infantry in 1860; and retired as colonel 3rd March, 1890. He married Frances Fitzgerald, of Dublin.

7. ELLEN AMY, married to Major-General George Carr Hodding, C.B., Madras Staff Corps, who died 19th January, 1894.

8. ALICE, married 10th January, 1864, to Colonel Herbert Augustus Tierney Nepean, Madras Staff Corps, and was divorced in 1878.

9. EDITH, married to M. Lecoe, of Paris and Madras, banker.

10. HENRIETTA, married to Colonel Butler, Madras Native Infantry.

11. SAMUEL, emigrated to Colorado.

12. FLORENCE, not married.

# BIBLIOGRAPHICAL APPENDIX.

### CORNWALL BAYLEY.

(1) Epigrammata numismate annuo dignata et in curia Cantabrigiensi recitata, A.D. 1802. Auctore Cornwall Bayley, Coll. Christ. 8vo, pp. 4.

(2) Helvetiorum luctus et querimoniae. [Greek verse.] Signed "Cornwall Bayley, Coll. Christ. Schol. 1803. *Musæ Cantabrigiensis*, Lond. 1810. pp. 156-162.

(3) Σκηνὲ πᾶς ὁ βίος. [Greek and Latin verse.] Signed "Cornwall Bayley, Coll. Christi, 1802." *Ibid.* pp. 211, 212.

### HENRY VINCENT BAYLEY, D.D.

(1) Oratio priore praemiorum senioribus baccalaureis annuo propositorum donata et in curia Cantabrigiensi recitata A.D. 1802. Mancunii: Excudebant C. Wheeler et Filius. 4to, pp. 13.

> The dedication is as follows: " Memoriae Patris desideratissimi hoc qualecunque opusculum ipsius jussi conscriptum dicari voluit pietatis ergo auctor filius H. V. B."

(2) A Sermon preached at an ordination held in the Cathedral Church of Chester, September 25th, 1803. By the Rev. H. V. Bayley, A.M., Fellow of Trinity College, Cambridge, and Chaplain to the Lord Bishop of Chester. Manchester: Printed by C. Wheeler and Son. 8vo, pp. [iv] 16.

(3a) A Charge delivered to the Clergy of the Archdeaconry of Stow, at the Visitation in May, 1826. By Henry Vincent Bayley, D.D., Archdeacon of Stow. Gainsborough, printed. for the author, by Adam Stark. MDCCCXXVI. 8vo, pp. 49.

(3*b*) A Charge delivered to the Clergy of the Archdeaconry of Stow, at the Visitation in May, 1826. By Henry Vincent Bayley, D.D., Archdeacon of Stow. Gainsborough, printed by Adam Stark. MDCCCXXVII. 8vo, pp. 51.

A Memoir of Henry Vincent Bayley, D.D. [By C. W. Le Bas.] Printed for Private Circulation. 1846. 8vo, pp. 66.

### HENRY VINCENT BAYLEY, H.E.I.C.S.

Dorjé-ling. "Te flagrantis atrox hora caniculae nescit tangere." *Hor.* Calcutta: G. H. Hullmann, Bengal Military Orphan Press. 1838. 8vo, pp. ii 57, vii. 10, 8, xxxi. xiv. iii. v.

Preface signed "H. V. Bayley, Political Department."

### THOMAS BUTTERWORTH BAYLEY.

(1) On a cheap and expeditious method of draining land. Hunter's *Georgical Essays*, 1772, vol. iv.; and reprinted in 1803 edition, vol. i., pp. 492-502.

(2) Observations on the general Highway and Turnpike Acts passed in the seventh year of His present Majesty; and also upon the report of the Committee of the House of Commons, who were appointed upon the twenty-eighth of April, 1772, to consider the above acts. London: Printed for Joseph Johnson, No. 72, St. Paul's Church-Yard, MDCCLXXIII. 8vo.

(3) A Charge delivered to the Grand Jury on the opening of the New Bayley Court House, at the Quarter Sessions at Manchester, April 22nd, 1790. By Thomas B. Bayley. Manchester, 1790. 4to, pp. 14.

(4) Rules, Orders, and Bye-Laws for the government of the House of Correction and Penitentiary house (commonly called the New Bayley Prison). 1794. 4to, pp. 19.

Signed by Thomas B. Bayley, chairman, and other magistrates.

(5) Plans and descriptions of Single-horse Carts, communicated to Thomas B. Bayley, Esq., by Dr. James Anderson and the Rev. Thomas Gisborne; and printed by order of the general meeting of the Agricultural Society at Manchester, August 3rd, 1795, for the use of members of the Society. Manchester: printed at G. Nicholson and Co.'s office, Palace-street, 1795. 8vo., pp. 16.

With additions by T. B. Bayley.

(6a) Thoughts on the necessity and advantages of care and œconomy in collecting and preserving different substances for manure (addressed to the members of the Agricultural Society of Manchester). Likewise, the report of the committee of the Board of Agriculture, respecting Mr. Elkington's Mode of Drainage, etc. Manchester: Printed at G. Nicholson and Co.'s office, 4, Palace-street. 1795. 8vo, pp. 18.

(6b) Thoughts [etc., as above]. By Thomas B. Bayley, F.R.S., and Honorary Member of the Board of Agriculture in London. The Second edition, with additions. Manchester: Printed and sold by George Nicholson, 9, Spring Gardens; sold also by T. Knott, 47, Lombard-street, London; and by all other booksellers. 1796. 8vo, pp. 23.

(6c) Thoughts [etc., as in second edition]. The Third edition, with additions. Manchester: Printed by C. Wheeler and Son, Cannon-street; of whom it may be had, and of Mess. Clarke, Booksellers, in the Market-Place. 1799. 8vo, pp. 24.

(7) A Charge delivered to the Grand Jury at the Quarter Sessions, at the New Bayley Court-House, in Salford, April the twenty-fifth, 1798. By Thomas Butterworth Bayley, Esq., Chairman. Printed at the request of the Grand Jury. Second edition. Manchester: Printed by C. Wheeler and Son, Cannon-street; of whom it may be had, and of Mess. Clarke, Booksellers, in the Market-Place. 1799. 8vo, pp. 12.

Biographical Memoirs of the late Thomas Butterworth Bayley, Esq., F.R.S., &c., &c., of Hope Hall, near Manchester. [By Thomas Percival, M.D.] Manchester:

Printed by W. Shelmerdine and Co. 1802. Sm. 4to, pp. 12.

Reprinted, with additions, in Dr. Percival's "Works." Bath. 1807. Vol. II. pp. 287-305.

## WILLIAM BUTTERWORTH BAYLEY.

(1) On the advantages to be derived from an academical institution in India; considered in a moral, literary, and political point of view. By Mr. W. B. Bayley. *Essays by the Students of the College of Fort William, in Bengal.* Calcutta 1802. 8vo, pp. 35-46.

(2*a*) Thesis pronounced at the Disputation in the Hindoostanee language, on the sixth of February, 1802. By Mr W. B. Bayley. *Ibid*, pp. 207-220.

(2*b*) Translation of the foregoing Thesis. Position. The Hindoostanee is the most generally useful language in India. *Ibid*, pp. 220-228.

(3) A faithful history of the late discussions in Bengal, on the power of transportation without trial, assumed as a right by the supreme Government of India, to be exercised on any Englishman who may honestly avail himself of the Freedom of the Press, as by law established, with copies of the Official Correspondence between W. B. Bayley, Esq., Chief Secretary to Government, and Mr. Buckingham, the late Editor of the *Calcutta Journal.* Calcutta, February 25th, 1823. Sm. fol. pp. 228.

## WILLIAM HENRY BAYLEY.

(1) Selections from the Records of the Madras Government. Published by authority. No. viii. Proposed plan for the Revenue Assessment of Kurnool in the year 1843. Madras: Printed by H. Smith, at the Fort St. George Gazette Press, 1854. 8vo, pp. [iv] 76.

(2) Memorandum on the Land-Measures of the Madras Presidency, and Memorandum on the Weights and Measures

of the Madras Presidency. [Signed, W. H. Bayley, member of the Board of Revenue. pp. 98, xxxvi.

(3*a*) Handbook of the Slide Rule, shewing its applicability to i. Arithmetic (including interest and annuities), ii. Mensuration (superficial and solid, including land surveying). With numerous examples & useful tables. By W. H. Bayley, H.M. East India Civil Service. London: Bell and Daldy, 1861. 8vo, pp. xii, 340.

(3*b*) Handbook [etc., as in first edition]. New revised edition. London: Geo. Bell and Sons, 1876. 8vo, pp. xii, 328.

(4) Papers on Mirasi Right. Selected from the Records of Government and published by permission. Madras: Pharaoh & Co., Athenæum Press, Mount Road. 1862. 8vo, pp. vii, 590, xxiv., xi., xl., xxiii.

> Begun by W. H. Bayley and completed by W. Hudleston.

(5) Handbook of the "Double" Slide Rule, shewing its applicability to navigation. Including some remarks on great circle sailing and variation of the compass, with useful astronomical memoranda. By W. H. Bayley, (late) H.M. East India Civil Service. London: Bell & Daldy. 1864. 8vo, pp. ii, 137.

(6) Indian Coinage and Accounts. By W. H. Bayley, Esq., of the Madras Civil Service. W. A. Browne's *Merchant's Handbook*, 1872. Appendix I. pp. i-vii.

# NOTES.

1. *Authorities.*—This pedigree of the Bayley family is founded to some extent on a MS. pedigree compiled by the Rev. Joseph Hunter, from the information of Mr. Gamaliel Lloyd, and now in the British Museum (Add. MSS. 24, 458, f. 66), which has been recently printed by the Harleian Society, and with a few additions by the late Mr. Croston in his edition of Baines's *History of Lancashire.* Additional facts as to the early generations are taken from the MSS. of Mr. John Owen, from an unpublished pedigree compiled by Mr. John Eglington Bailey, from Mr. J. Fred Beever's paper in *Local Gleanings,* i. 103, 166, from the Manchester Court Leet Records and Constable's Accounts, and from a pedigree in the Piccope MSS. in Chetham's Library. The facts concerning the later generations have been obtained from the members of the family who are named in the preface.

2. *Origin of the Family.*—I have been unable to trace the family beyond the seventeenth century. The name was by no means uncommon in Lancashire and Cheshire at that time. A family tradition, dating apparently from the date of Thomas Butterworth Bayley's stay in Edinburgh, that the Bayleys were descended from a cadet of the Baillies of Linlithgowshire, does not seem to have any foundation in fact, the family having been established in Manchester long before the date assigned for the migration. Mr. J. E. Bailey was of opinion that Thomas Bayley, the first known member of the family, was a native of the neighbourhood of Blackburn, but I do not know on what authority he based his opinion. It is worth mentioning that the unusual spelling of the name is not a recent adoption, but has always been used by the members of the family since the time of Thomas Bayley, who died in 1688.

# INDEX.

The contractions s., d., and w. are used in this index for "son of," "daughter of," and "wife of," respectively.

Ainsworth, W. Harrison 7
Barlow, Frances 47
—— John 47
Bayley, Adelaide d. Francis 49
—— Adeline Anne d. Henry Vincent 37
—— Alice d. Thomas 2
—— Alice d. Daniel 3
—— Alice d. James Walker 50
—— Alice Janet Clive d. Sir E. C. 31
—— Alice Mary d. Charles Stuart 34
—— Alicia Fenton d. William Henry 26
—— Alicia Sidney d. Sir Steuart C. 36
—— Amelia Maria w. Edward Henry 35
—— Amy Ann d. James 48
—— Amy Steuart d. Edward Henry 35
—— Ann w. Thomas 2
—— Anna w. Sir Steuart C. 35
—— Annabella Maxwell w. James Walker 50
—— Anne d. Thomas 2
—— Anne d. Daniel 3
—— Anne d. James 39
—— Anne d. Samuel 39
—— Anne d. Thomas 45
—— Anne Augusta w. William Butterworth 33
—— Annie Margaret Clive d. Sir E. C. 30
—— Appylina d. James 40
—— Arabella d. James 40
—— Archibald s. Francis S. 49
—— Archibald Stuart Butterworth s. Charles Stuart 34

Bayley, Ariana w. Henry 37
—— Charles s. Thomas B. 24
—— Charles Butterworth s. Sir Steuart C. 36
—— Charles Septimus s. Francis S. 49
—— Charles Stuart s. Daniel 34
—— Charles Theophilus Richard Clive s. Sir E. C. 31
—— Charlotte Anstruther Canning Clive d. Sir E. C. 31
—— Clive Christian s. Francis S. 49
—— Clive Campbell s. Sir Steuart C. 36
—— Clive William s. Sir Steuart C. 35
—— Cornwall s. Thomas B. 27, 51
—— Daniel s. Thomas 2
—— Daniel s. James 6, 7
—— Daniel (Sir) s. Thomas B. 19
—— Daniel (Captain) s. William Butterworth 34
—— Daniel Benjamin s. Daniel 13
—— Diggles s. James 47
—— Edith d. James Walker 50
—— Edward Clive s. Thomas B. 21, 28
—— Edward Clive (Sir) s. Edward Clive 28, 29
—— Edward Henry s. William Butterworth 35
—— Edward Metcalfe Clive s. Sir E. C. 31
—— Eleanor w. Sir Daniel 20
—— Eleanor Louisa d. Edward Clive 28

I

Bayley, Elizabeth d. Daniel 3
—— Elizabeth d. Daniel 10
—— Elizabeth d. James 39
—·—· Elizabeth d. James 39
—— Elizabeth d. Thomas 45
—— Elizabeth Cathcart d. Edward
  Clive 28
—·— Ellen d. Francis S. 49
—— Ellen Amy d. James Walker 50
—— Emily Anne Theophila w. Sir
  Edward Clive 30
—— Emily Isabella Clive d. Sir E. C.
  30
—  Esther w. Samuel 42
—·— Esther d. Thomas 44
—— Ethel Augusta Colvin d. Sir
  Steuart C. 36
—— Ethel Hermione d. Charles
  Stuart 34
—— Florence d. James Walker 50
—  Florence Tempe d. Charles
  Stuart 34
—— Frances d. Daniel 12
—— Frances d. Thomas B. 24
—  Frances d. James 40
—— Frances w. Rev. James 41
—·— Frances d. James 47
—·· Frances w. Henry Elliott Dash-
  wood 50
—·— Frances Cumming d. Edward
  Clive 28
——  Frances Mary Lushington d.
  Sir Steuart C. 36
—·  Frances Ralston d. James
  Walker 50
—— Francis s. Samuel 48
—·— Francis Price s. Francis S. 49
—·— Francis Samuel s. Francis 49
—·— Frederick s. Thomas B. 27
—·— Frederic Hamilton s. Charles 26
—·— Gilbert s. Thomas 45
—·· George Anson s. Francis S. 49
—·— GeorgeThornton s. Thomas B. 27
—·— Georgiana Charlotte Clive d.
  Sir E. C. 31
—  Hannah w. Henry Vincent 7, 23
—  Hannah d. Samuel 42
—— Harriet w. Diggles 47
—— Harriet Anne w. Samuel 48

Bayley, Harriet Parr d. Samuel 48
—— Harriet Stuart d. William
  Butterworth 33
—— Helen Eliza w. of Cornwall 27
—— Henrietta w. William Henry 26
—— Henrietta d. James Walker 50
—·· Henrietta Elizabeth d. William
  Henry 26
—— Henrietta Frances d. Charles 24
—·—· Henrietta Frances d. William
  Butterworth 34
—— Henry s. Henry Vincent 37
—— Henry s. Samuel Henry 48
—·— Henry Cornwall s. Thomas B. 21
—— Henry Elliott Dashwood s.
  James Walker 50
—·— Henry Vincent, D.D. s. Thomas
  B. 21, 51
—·— Henry Vincent s. William
  Butterworth 33, 36, 52
—·— Hugh s. Francis S. 49
—·— Isabel w. William Kennedy 45
—  Isabel Constance d. Charles
  Stuart 34
—·— Isabella Frances w. Captain
  Daniel 34
—·· Isabella Tempe d. Daniel 34
—— James s. Daniel 3, 4
—— James s. James 6, 38
—·— James s. Daniel 12
—·— James s. James 39
—·— James (Rev.) s. James 39, 40
—  James s. Samuel 42
—·  James s. Samuel 43, 46
—·— James s. James 47
—·— James Crawford s. James Walker
  50
—— James Diggles s. James 47
—·· James Reginald s. James
  Crawford 50
—·— James Walker s. Samuel 48, 49
—· Jane d. James 39
—·— Janie w. William Clements 50
—·— John s. James 6
—— John s. Thomas B. 21
—·— John s. James 39
—·— John s. Samuel 43
—·— John Diggles s. Thomas 45
—·— John Parr s. Francis S. 49

Bayley, Katharine d. Francis S. 49
—— Kate d. James Walker 50
—— Kate Sainton Clive d. Sir E. C.
31
—— Lionel Seton s. Sir Steuart C. 36
—— Louisa w. Henry Vincent 37
—— Lucy Seely d. William Henry 26
—— Lucy Wilton d. Charles 25
—— Lytton Cecil Lambert s. Sir
Steuart C. 36
—— Mabel Elliott Clive d. Sir E.C. 31
—— Margaret w. Edward Clive 28
—— Margaret w. James 46
—— Margaret d. James 47
—— Maria Barbara w. Sir Daniel 20
—— Marion Hamilton d. Sir Steuart
C. 36
—— Mary d. Thomas 2
—— Mary w. Thomas Butterworth 19
—— Mary d. Sir Daniel 20
—— Mary d. Cornwall 27
—— Mary d. James 39
—— Mary d. James 39
—— Mary w. Thomas 43
—— Mary d. Thomas 44
—— Mary d. James Walker 50
—— Mary Amy d. Francis S. 49
—— Mary Ann w. Francis 49
—— Mary Ann w. James Walker 50
—— Mary Anne d. Thomas B. 21
—— Mary Anne w. Charles 24
—— Mary Anne d. Charles 24
—— Mary Elizabeth Jane w. Francis
S. 49
—— Mary Louisa d. Francis 49
—— Mary Margaret d. Edward Clive
28
—— Mary Steuart d. William Butter-
worth 34
—— Mary Theophila Steuart Clive
d. Sir E. C. 31
—— May d. Henry 37
—— Melvill Gordon s. Sir Steuart C.
36
—— Mia Louisa d. Henry Vincent 37
—— Norah Lilian d. Sir Steuart C. 36
—— Robert Riddell s. Thomas 45
—— Samuel s. James 6, 42
—— Samuel s. James 39

Bayley, Samuel s. Thomas 43
—— Samuel s. James 47, 48
—— Samuel s. James Walker 50
—— Samuel Henry s. Samuel 48
—— Sarah d. Thomas 2
—— Sarah w. Daniel 3
—— Sarah d. Daniel 3
—— Sarah d. James 6
—— Sarah d. Daniel 13
—— Sarah d. Thomas B. 20
—— Sarah d. James 38
—— Sarah d. Samuel 43
—— Sarah d. Thomas 44
—— Sarah Constance w. Charles
Stuart 34
—— Steuart Colvin (Sir) s. William
Butterworth 35
—— Steuart Farquharson s. Sir
Steuart C. 35
—— Susannah d. Daniel 13
—— Theresa Selina Clive d. Sir E.
C. 31
—— Thomas 1
—— Thomas s. Thomas 2
—— Thomas s. Samuel 43
—— Thomas Butterworth s. Daniel
13, 52
—— Thomas Butterworth s. Edward
Clive 28
—— Thomas Butterworth Charles s.
Charles 25
—— Thomas Diggles s. Thomas 44
—— Thomas Dukinfield s. Thomas
B. 27
—— Thomas Leggatt s. Thomas B.
20
—— Thomas Wilton s. Charles 24
—— Timothy s. Thomas 2
—— William Butterworth s. Thomas
Butterworth 27, 32, 54
—— William Butterworth Master s.
William Butterworth 34
—— William Clements s. James
Walker 50
—— William de l'Etang s. Henry
Vincent 37
—— William Eden s. Sir Steuart C.
36
—— William Henry s. Charles 25, 54

Bayley, William Kennedy s. Thomas 44, 45
—— William Kennedy s. William Kennedy 45
— — Wilton Rees s. Charles 25
Bigg-Wither, Frank 50
—— Kate 50
Booth, Sir Robert 10
Bradshaw, Rev. James 3
—— Sarah 3
Broome, Frances 41
—— Richard 41
Browne, Felicite Anne, 30
—— John 30
Burns, Robert 44, 45
Butler, Colonel 50
—— Henrietta 50
Butterworth, Ann 8
—— Anne 10
—— Thomas 10
Campbell, General Archibald E. 34
—— Henrietta Frances 34
—— John Scarlett 35
—— Lilian 35
—— Sarah Constance 34
—— William 35
Chapman, Major-General E. F. 31
—— Georgiana C. C. 31
Churton, Ann 2
Clive, Robert (Lord) 8
—— Robert, M.P. 8
Colvin, Bazett David 34
—— Elliot Graham 36
—— Ethel A. C. 36
—— Mary Steuart 34
—— Sidney 34
—— William 34
Crawfurd, Annabella Maxwell 50
Crowther, Ann 10
Diggles, Esther 43
—— James 43
—— Thomas 43
Dyas, James Jones 27
—— Mary 27
—— Richard 27
—— Richard Hudson 27
Dukinfield, Frances 10
—— Sir Robert 10
Edge, Hannah 42

Edge, William 42
Elton, Ellen 49
—— Henry 49
Emmet, Amelia Maria 35
—— Edward 35
Every Family 39
Farquharson, Anna 35
—— Robert N. 35
Feilden Family 39
Fenton, James 28
—— Margaret 28
ffarington, Mrs. 7
Fitzgerald, Frances 50
Fock, Maria Barbara 26
Fowler, Alan Arthur 31
—— Alice J. C. 31
—— Sir John 31
—— John Arthur 31
—— John Edward 31
—— Mabel Elizabeth 31
—— Marjorie Theophila 31
Gaskell, Elizabeth 8
—— Nathaniel 8
Gaussen, Alice Ada Sophia 26
—— Alicia Fenton 26
—— Charles 26
—— James Robert 26
Greg, Lucy 44
—— William R. 44
Gladstone, Alicia Sidney 36
—— William Buckley 36
Haddon, Appylina 40
—— Giles F. 40
Hamilton, Captain 47
—— Frances 47
Harris, Amy Steuart 35
—— James Alfred, M.D. 35
Harrison, J. Bower 7
—— Rev. John, Ph.D. 7
Henry, Lucy 44
—— Mary 44
—— William 44
— — William Charles 44
Hibbert, Esther 42
—— Robert 42
Hodding, Ellen Amy 50
—— George Carr 50
Hodson, James 47
—— Margaret 46

Hoghton, Lady 10
Jackson, Anne Augusta 33
—— William 33
Joddrell, Mrs. 10
Johnson, Colonel 50
—— Mary 50
Jones, Helen Eliza 27
Kennedy, Mary 43
—— William 43
Kibble, Hervey 49
—— Mary Louisa 49
Kirkes, Samuel 6
—— Sarah 6
Lecoe, M. 50
—— Edith 50
Leggatt, Mary 19
—— Vincent 19
Le Marchand, Ariana 37
Lever, Sir Ashton 40
—— Frances (Lady) 40
Lubbock, Montagu, M.D. 37
—— Nora 37
Macnamara, Adeline Louisa 37
—— Charles C. 37
—— Dorothy Mia 37
—— Maive 37
—— Mia Louisa 37
—— Nora 37
—— Nottidge C. 37
—— Oona 37
—— Patrick Guy 37
—— Sheila 37
Mactier Adeline 37
—— Adeline Anne 37
—— Adeline Harris 37
—— Anthony D. 37
—— Charles B. 37
—— Henry M. 37
—— Maria Louisa 37
—— Minnie Moir 37
—— Thomas B. 37
—— William B. 37
—— William F. 37
Master Family 39
Metcalfe, Charles (Lord) 30
—— Cornelius 43
—— Emily Anne Theophila 30
—— Sarah 43
—— Sir Thomas Theophilus 30

Mosley, Sir Edward 10
—— Elizabeth (Lady) 39
—— Sir John P. 39
Moss, Appylina 40
—— James 40
Murray, Janie 50
Nepean, Alice 50
—— Herbert A. T. 50
Oakes, Isabella Frances 34
—— William Henry 34
Oldfield, Charles Bayley 26
—— Frederick Biscoe 26
—— Rev. George B. 26
—— Gertrude Letitia 26
—— Henrietta 26
—— Henry Swann 26
Ottley, Henrietta 26
—— William Young 26
Palmer, E. G. 47
—— Harriet 47
Pattle, James 37
—— Louisa 37
Peploe, Anne 38
—— Bishop Samuel 38
Phelan, Mary Ann 50
Pirie, Harold Victor C. 35
—— Lilian 35
—— Martin Henry 35
—— Wilfrid Bayley 35
Potter, Esther (Lady) 44
—— Sir John 44
—— Sir Thomas 44
—— Thomas Bayley 44
Price, John Thomas 49
—— Mary Elizabeth Jane 49
Railton, Adelaide Frances 49
—— William 49
Rasbotham, Dorning 38
—— Sarah 38
Ricketts, Edward Wallace Claud 30
—— Emily Isabella Clive 30
—— George Henry Mildmay 30
Riddell, Mrs. Robert 45
Ridley, Mrs. N. J. 7
Rouse, Adeline Louisa 37
—— Hubert 37
Russell Isabel 45
—— John 45
Saffree, Eleanor 20

Sempill, Hon. Mrs. George 10
—— Hugh (Lord) 8
Shaw, David 50
—— Frances Ralston 50
Smith, Edward Peploe 24
—— Henrietta Frances 24
—— Mary Anne 24
Smyth, David S. C. 34
Standen, Bertram Prior 37
——- Oona 37
Taylor, John 49
—— Mary Ann 49

Touchet, Hannah 7, 23
-—— James 23
-—— John 6
-—-· Sarah 6
Walker, Harriet Anne 48
—— Jane 39
—— Richard 48
-—-- Rev. Thomas 40
Wall, Miss 39
Ward, Abel 39
—— Anne 39
Wilton, John 24

MANCHESTER:
PRINTED BY RICHARD GILL, TIB LANE,
CROSS STREET.